Weird Thoughts

By
Thomas Wm. Hamilton

Strategic Book Publishing and Rights Co.

Strategic Book Publishing and Rights Co., LLC
USA | Singapore

For information about special discounts for bulk purchases, please contact Strategic Book Publishing and Rights Co. Special Sales, at bookorder@sbpra.net.

ISBN: 978-1-946540-77-5

Book Design: Suzanne Kelly

TABLE OF CONTENTS

Part One: Fiction?

This story is based on an actual historical event, the murder during a robbery of California State Assembly member John E. Mullally, January 14, 1912, as documented in various San Francisco newspapers. I've mainly based the story on the version in the San Francisco Call of January 15 et seq. All the named down timers are documented. Borrowed from Isaac Asimov the idea a culture could have space travel or time travel, but not both.

TIMELY MISADVENTURE

New York City, 2070

"Oh, scrunchies, President Miller just appointed a new governor for New York. Our citizenship classes will be filled with this junk." The morning news usually did not distract the teenager from concentrating on breakfast.

"Now Herbert, " his mother said, "you're only in tenth grade. You don't have the judgment yet to understand what's important. And I wish you wouldn't use such language. Just eat your breakfast!"

"And" his father added, "I hope you're smart enough to fol-low the teacher's lead and not open your mouth." He sipped some coffee.

"Yeah, but I like science, especially bio, not that citizenship junk. Let's see, the President loves us, but you can't criticize him or doubt his policies, bad people do that, and they disap-pear. Almost all foreigners are bad people. See, I already know everything from citizenship class." Herbert took a few bites of breakfast as a reward for his scholarly analysis.

"So much for heredity determining interests. And I hope you're smart enough never to make such comments outside home." Mother was frowning.

"Huh? Heredity?"

3

"You had a relative more than 150 years ago who was a member of the California state legislature. His name was Mullally, on my side of the family, not your father's Crenshaw side. Unfortunately he was murdered."

"President's orders?"

"No, he was trying to stop a hold up."

~~~

Offices of Timely Adventures, Inc., 2087

"Ah, Mr. Herbert Crenshaw right on time for your appointment. Welcome to Timely Adventures, Incorporated. Have you seen our brochures or website?"

"Yes, but unfortunately I don't speak Latin or some other language whose adventures look intriguing. So I'm limited to English speaking places and times. I finally narrowed it to New Orleans before it was shut down during the First World War, or San Francisco during the wide open period of rebuilding following the big 1906 earthquake."

"And have you chosen between those, or could we help advise you?" The salesman gave an unctuous grin as he contemplated the surcharge associated with advisement.

"I flipped a coin, and San Francisco won."

The salesman's expression lost a bit of its grin. "A choice I'm sure you'll be happy with. Have you a particular date in mind for arrival? And how long would you wish to visit there?"

"Let's say arrive on December 29, 1911 so I have enough time to find a good New Year's Eve party. And I can afford to pay for three weeks, which I guess means through January 18, 1912."

"Very good. You know you won't be able to take anything back with you but a suitcase to hold clothing, and cash of the period, all of which we provide, the cost included in your charges. You must have innoculations against what were then endemic diseases, most of which you've probably never heard of, such as polio and typhoid. And anything other than the suitcase, clothing and left over cash that you bring back will be impounded until federal officials have cleared it. You can leave from here, but returns are always from the reception center nearest to the place you have been visiting. That's for the convenience of the government people who check for changes in the timeline."

"No problem, I'm just looking for a good time, not for messing with history or smuggling in art or something."

"What's your occupation?"

"I'm a freelance writer specializing in topics related to oceanography, Writer's License 551-V16-27497 C45, issued by the Federal Writers Authority on June 8, 2081."

The salesman entered this into his computer to verify his claim. "You know you are _not_ to tell anyone in your occupation in 1911 any advance information."

"The field was just beginning to become a science then. I don't know of anyone working in it in the San Francisco area back then, but don't worry, I'm looking for fun, not trying to teach people who probably wouldn't believe me."

"Excellent." He tapped his computer. "I see only five residents of the San Francisco area in 1911 named Crenshaw. Two seem never to have had children, and the family name of the others daughtered out within a couple generations. What was your mother's maiden name?"

"Hoefherr." He spelled it.

"Humph, looks like no one in the entire state with that name until the 1930s. Alright, complete these forms, and we'll have you in 1911 before you know it."

Crenshaw looked at the thickness of the packet and gulped. "All this?"

"It includes various waivers, as we are not responsible for what happens to you 176 years ago, only for getting you there and back, and you agree not to make any significant changes in the time line. The packet includes a requirement you reveal any personal connections to the time and place visited."

"What kind of connection could I have to a time 143 years before my birth, in a city I've never seen in any time?"

"You would be surprised at what some people have tried. Anyhow, just fill out the forms, pay, and we'll have you celebrating the New Year of 1912 in the city by the bay before you know it."

Crenshaw spent half an hour reading and signing the various forms, including one indicating he was aware that deliberately or even accidentally making noticeable changes to the timeline was a federal offense punishable by anything up to and including death.

He reported to Timely Adventures' transfer station two days later, filled with injections blocking a host of diseases, most of which, as predicted, he had never heard of. He also was temporarily sterilized, so he could not mess with the timeline by creating children during any sex romps. Crenshaw changed into clothing appropriate for San Francisco in late 1911, and was given a wallet containing $420 in early Twentieth Century American currency, plus a couple dollars in pocket change. "You'll get a refund for any money you return unspent."

"This doesn't seem like much money for carousing for three weeks."

"Prices were very different in 1911. This is roughly equal to thirty thousand dollars today."

"Wow! I'll have to be careful no one cheats me on prices."

"Never a bad idea, in any time or place. Do you have a specific location in San Francisco in mind for the transfer?"

"Not really. Anywhere in the downtown district would be convenient. I assume you won't have me suddenly appear out of nowhere at noon on Market Street. Maybe a dark alley near a hotel?"

~~~

San Francisco, December 29, 1911

Crenshaw examined his surroundings. He appeared to be in a dark alley behind some sort of fairly large building. He slipped out onto a street with a number of men and women dressed in period clothing walking about. Some horse drawn carriages and

6

ridiculously primitive looking cars completed the archaic scene. Looking back at the building, he saw it was still under construction. A sign proclaimed it the future home of the Olympic Club. The horses seemed to contribute to the city's aroma. He waited for a moment until a reasonably peaceful looking man came by, and stopped him. "Excuse me sir, I'm a stranger here, and I'm looking for Eighth Street. Could you point me in the right direction?"

"Eighth Street, eh? I'm betting you'd be looking for Mullally's saloon on the corner of Minna. Politics or beer?"

"I'll gladly start with the beer; I've little interest in politics, Mullally's or anyone else's."

"Don't let his sister Mary hear yuh say that, or she'll chew your ears off arguing. She's one o' them suffragettes. Yuh know what a suffragette is, don't yuh? A loudmouth woman what makes everyone else suffer." He guffawed.

Crenshaw politely chuckled, followed by thanks after getting the requested directions. As he crossed Seventh Street he saw a house with a sign:

Rooms for Rent
$5 to $7 per Week
No Salesmen, Drunks or Gospel Shouters
White Men Only

"Perfect for me, " Crenshaw said to himself, "but I wonder which would create a bigger riot back home, the prices or that last line." He knocked on the door.

"Yeah?" The man answering the door was short, a bit stout, and in need of a shave.

"I'm interested in one of your better rooms for three weeks, and I'm not a salesman, drunk or gospel shouter. In fact, I'm usually pretty soft spoken."

7

"No $7 rooms available. $6 room has bed, chair, closet. Five bucks don't have the chair. You can use the outhouse in back like everyone else, including me. Pay for a week now."

"Fine with me. I'll only be staying until January 18, and if you like, I'll pay for all three weeks now."

"You leave early, no refund."

"That's okay, I don't expect to leave early."

"You sure you ain't no gospel shouter or one o' them political ajeetaytors? You talk pretty fancy."

"I'm from Back East. I talk pretty normal for there." He handed $18 to the man, who carefully counted it twice, and pocketed the cash without a thank you. He waved for Crenshaw to follow him into the building. The room was shown, a key handed over. After the owner left Crenshaw put down the suitcase he had been carrying, and sat in the room's sole chair, relaxing for a moment. He looked around at the room. A soiled curtain over the window probably had not been cleaned since the Earthquake of 1906. The chair he sat in had little to recommend it, unless one enjoyed risking splinters. The bedding at least was almost clean. "Good thing I'm so loaded with medical protection."

After putting the suitcase unopened in the closet, Crenshaw left the room. He carefully locked the door. A couple blocks back he had spotted a shop carrying one of the two purchases he intended. That was his next destination.

A clerk looked up as he walked in. "Yes, sir, may I help you?"

"I'm looking for an inexpensive but dependable handgun, one that can fire multiple shots before reloading, and is accurate to at least thirty feet.

"We have several models in stock. Would you care to see them?"

"Definitely. A choice improves chances for something I like."

The clerk placed a rather odd looking gun with an enormous wooden stock on the counter. "This is a Mauser C96, made in Germany, holds ten rounds in that boxy thing in front of the trigger guard, and comes with either 7.65 mm or 9 mm ammunition."

"The stock looks much too clunky for me. Let's try an American make, if you have any."

"Even the Army uses versions of the Colt. These are the 1902 Sporting model and the 1911 model the Army recently adopted. Both are widely used by civilians, and fire well without jamming if you are dependable about cleaning them after each use. They hold seven rounds, and use .45 caliber ammunition. The 1911 has a four and seven-eighth inch long barrel for added accuracy."

"How much?"

"The Sporting model is $14.25, and the 1911 is a bit more. The ammunition comes boxed, 40 to a box, and one box is included in the price."

Crenshaw picked up each of the guns and examined it, flicking open and checking to see how the bullets were loaded in. "I'll take the Sporting model, and one box of ammunition." He took out his wallet, and got out fifteen dollars, which he handed to the clerk. The clerk took the money, counted out his change, and then put the Colt and box of bullets in a bag.

"The city police tend to get interested in people who walk around displaying a gun too openly."

"That's okay, it's not like I'm wanted in all forty six states plus Canada and Puerto Rico." He laughed. "But thanks for the warning. I'll take this back to my room and leave it there."

"A wise move. It has been a pleasure serving you. Should you need additional arms or more bullets, we'll be here."

"Would you know of any place near here that sells typewriters?"

"Hmm, I think there's a shop on Mission Street near Sixth sells the Williams brand as a sideline to doing printing. But you can just tell the people in the bank to hand over the money, you needn't type it."

"Huh? Oh, very funny. Anyhow, thanks for your help."

Crenshaw headed for the print shop, with the gun and ammo bagged under his arm. The typewriter cost him another $60, and he additionally purchased five cents worth of paper to type on. He carried everything back to his room, then went out to find someplace to eat. "Would saloons have food, or just alcohol? Now's the time to find out."

He headed for Eighth Street. The saloon he was interested in occupied a corner, and ran to nearly half the block. He went in and looked around. There was a long bar in the back of the room, with shelves full of bottles, mugs and glasses above it. Bar stools along the length of the bar, and about a dozen small tables with three or four chairs for each. Seven men were scattered with drinks across three of the tables. The left wall had a mural of some Roman or Greek style god standing in front of a cask, holding a wine glass, surrounded by maidens in decidedly diaphanous gowns. The right wall displayed a map of San Francisco, with part outlined in red, and a large "30" on the top. There was a buffet beneath the map with a sign saying "Free lunch with drinks you already paid for".

Crenshaw walked to the bar. "You Jack? Gimme your best beer."

"My fame reached you? Yep, I'm Jack Tierney. The beer's four bits."

Crenshaw handed him a dollar and said, "Keep the change. By the way, I'm Frank Bates."

"Pleased to meet you, Mr. Bates, keep spending like that and we'll be good friends."

"Assemblyman Mullally around?"

"Not yet. The legislature's home for the holidays, so he ain't in Sacramento, but he ain't come in here yet today. You got some politics you wanna talk with him?"

Crenshaw shuddered theatrically, and took a deep gulp of his beer. "God no. Spare me from all politicians. No, I was hoping to discuss protecting this place from the goons who've been doing all the stick ups near here."

"Yeah, I've been kind of nervous, since it looks like they're moving in this direction. You a gun salesman?"

"Don't you already have a gun behind that bar?"

"Sure, and I can load it in less than a minute."

"Excuse me for saying this, but that's the damned stupidest thing I've heard so far today. Those goons come in here, they can have you dead in a lot less than a minute, 'cause they sure as hell got their guns already loaded. Keep the damn thing loaded."

A man sitting nearby added, "Yeah Jack, and if Bob here can't hold his liquor, you could bop him with your gun. That's about all an unloaded gun is good for."

Crenshaw turned to face the new speaker, and gave him a thumbs up. A second man, presumably Bob, said, "Hey Gilroy, you're the one can't hold his liquor. I saw how you staggered out o' here last Saturday."

The room dissolved into an open discussion among the patrons as to who was best or least capable of holding his liquor. Crenshaw turned back to the bartender and said in a low voice, "I'm serious, keep the gun loaded, and don't be afraid to use it if they show up here. Those goons are very dangerous." He took another drink, and added, "This beer's not bad." He walked over to the "free lunch". A large ham with a sharp knife, a darker meat that may have been venison, fragments of a chicken, several kinds of cheese, some sausages, tomatoes, apples, grapes, deviled eggs, sourdough bread, a cake, a pie already sliced into. He grabbed a plate and helped himself.

The bartender said, "Mullally's wife made the cake and pie. She does that once or twice a week."

"Good for her. Does May ever make some sort of Portuguese specialties?"

Tierney stared at him. "You seem to know an awful lot for someone who just walked in here. Who the hell are you?"

"I'm a distant relative of Mullally. But we've never met. In fact, I've never been in San Francisco before today. Thought I'd get acquainted while I was in town."

Jack Tierney said, "Yeah, what kind of relative?"

"Sort of a nephew, but a lot more distant. Don't worry, I'm not looking for money or a job, or anything else. Just hoping to meet a relative who seems to be doing pretty well for himself."

The bartender grunted, and seemed to have lost interest in Crenshaw. To try to re-establish relations, he asked for another beer. Tierney plopped it in front of him without comment, even

11

when he again paid with a dollar. After slowly finishing his meal and second beer, Crenshaw hung around hoping Mullally might show up, but with Tierney getting progressively more hostile, decided to give up for the day. He returned to his room, where he typed for hours despite the awkward placement of the typewriter atop the suitcase mounted on his chair while he sat on the bed.

The next day he again showed up at the saloon around lunchtime. The "free lunch" was pretty much the same, except none of the pie remained, and a fresh chicken had been added. Tierney ignored him except to serve his beer and take his dollar. A few men wandered in and out with nothing remarkable happening until a man rather better dressed than most came in. He went to the back, where Tierney leaned over the bar and whispered to him. The man turned and stared at Crenshaw, then walked over to his table and sat down.

"Jack tells me you claim to be my nephew. You damn sure don't look like Bill, and he's the only nephew in town. What's your game?"

"You're Assemblyman John E. Mullally?"

"Yeah. And you?"

"I'm going by Frank Bates, because if what I'm about to tell you got back and was attributed to me, I'd almost certainly be executed when I go home. I'm not exactly a nephew, but we *are* distantly related."

"Uh huh, and what's this great secret? Got some blackmail worthy dirt on Assembly Speaker Hewitt? I might even be interested."

"No, it's about the gang that's been pulling all the robberies. They intend to hit this place on January 14."

"Son of a bitch! How do *you* know this?"

"We can't discuss this in public. You have a private place we can talk?"

"I've got a small office in back." He stood and gestured for Crenshaw to follow him.

Once they were seated in a room not much larger than a closet, with the door shut, Mullally began, "Alright, Bates, or whoever you are, what's this all about?"

Crenshaw began with, "This may sound irrelevant, but let me approach this my own way. Have you read much of Mark Twain's writings?"

"I got a good chuckle out of his essay on the German language, and I've read a few of his books. I guess we won't be getting more out of him. Why?"

"Have you read *A Connecticut Yankee in King Arthur's Court*?"

"No."

"How about H. G. Wells? *The Time Machine* to be specific?"

"I've seen some of his stuff. He seems to have pretty good politics for a Limey."

"You're not making this any easier to explain. I'm from the year 2087. I came back here supposedly as a tourist, but actually with the deliberate intention of preventing your murder during the hold up of this saloon on January 14, even though uptime such interference is regarded as an extremely serious criminal offense."

"Just how many beers did Jack serve you?"

"I wasn't allowed to bring anything back that might convince you, just what I could remember. I'm typing it up, so if we can assure you survive January 14, your political career goes a lot further."

"I suspect the priests at St. Joseph's would advise that I quote the Bible, 'Retro me, Satanas.'"

"Pfft. You're a good guy, but you're no Christ figure, and your Latin is flawed."

Mullally laughed. "Damn, but for no good reason I'm starting to believe you. So will Taft be re-elected next November?"

"No, he'll only come in third."

"Third! So who wins?"

"Woodrow Wilson."

"The Governor of New Jersey? But he's a Democrat."

"So? Democrats do win occasionally."

"Who comes in second?"

"Teddy Roosevelt."

"I seriously liked him as President, but if he decides to run against Taft, I can see how he'd split the vote and let a Democrat win. Damn, I'd much rather support TR than Taft, but not at the price of electing a Democrat! I'm starting to sound like I believe your nonsense."

"Whether you believe me or not, just make sure Tierney has that gun loaded. I'll be here on the Fourteenth to provide added firepower. Too bad effective bulletproof vests haven't been invented yet."

"Am I going to have to listen to you making comments like that? How long do you intend to hang around?"

"I return to my own time period on January 18."

"So I get one chance at living longer, and you won't be here to help after that."

Crenshaw shrugged. "I may have to check history books, or dig in old newspaper files, but I'll find out how well you will have done. That doesn't mean I can come back again to help you. It's damned expensive, plus the government may get suspicious if I spend too much time here."

"Why would the government care what you do in what you claim is your past?"

"Afraid of changing the world, of people setting up something so they are super-rich when they return to the present, of smuggling valuable art, all sorts of possibilities."

"I'm still not convinced you're not either crazy or trying to set up some scam. But I agree Jack should make sure that gun he keeps behind the bar is loaded, if that hold up gang may be headed this way."

Crenshaw gave a sigh. "On the Thirteenth I'm going to give you some typed notes that can help you in the future. But, two very important points. You must never let anyone else, your wife, anyone, ever see these notes or even know that they exist. Best if you burn the appropriate page as each thing they discuss is passed. And whatever happens on the Fourteenth, don't ever mention to the cops, newspapers, or anyone else that I was involved or even exist."

"Newspapers?"

"Any crime victimizing an elected official is sure to get lots of attention. That's as true in 2087 as it is in 1912."

Mullally continued to press "Bates" for his motives, while trying to decide if he really believed any of this. After an hour of conversation, he decided to end the discussion. "I'll tell Tierney to be polite. Don't press your luck by hanging around here every day, though." He stood, and directed Crenshaw out of his office. Following his advice, Crenshaw headed back to his room for more typing. He found a couple other venues for meals, and did not return to Mullally's saloon until January 13. He handed Mullally a thick typed manuscript, saying "It would probably be best if you don't start reading this until a few days from now. Tomorrow and most likely the day after the police may be keeping you busy investigating whatever happens with the crooks."

"You claimed you leave on the Eighteenth. I may want to ask you a few questions about whatever's in that pack."

"Alright, spend some time late on the Seventeenth reading, and I'll meet you in the morning before I go back, which should be at noon."

Late next evening Crenshaw placed himself at a table in a dark corner near the mural of the god sampling wine. He nodded approvingly when Mullally checked to see if Tierney's gun was loaded. Several customers sat around drinking and chatting. The door swung open to admit a large, muscular man with a white bandanna over his face and a gun in his hand. The phone on the bar started ringing as the man snarled, "Okay, you bastards, hands up."

Crenshaw, who had his gun resting in his lap, fired two shots. Two men with red bandannas over their faces entered. Mullally grabbed the weapon wielding arm of the first man as Tierney crouched behind the bar and fired at the second entrant. The third man fired wildly in Crenshaw's general direction, but missed. The second man returned Tierney's fire, smashing a couple bottles of whiskey. Crenshaw fired twice at the third man, who collapsed. The first one was now wrestling with Mullally despite bleeding profusely from his groin and thigh. One of the customers, all of whom had hit the floor, crawled to where the third man lay, grabbed the gun lying next to him. He and Crenshaw each shot the one exchanging gunfire with Tierney. Crenshaw tried to get another shot at the one wrestling with Mullally, but feared to hit Mullally. The customer, however, stood up, placed the gun right next to the man's head, and yelled "Give it up or I blow your brains out."

This criminal snarled several vile curses while still struggling with Mullally. A moment later his brains were scattered across the saloon.

The sudden silence was shocking. Mullally looked around calmly, and said, "Jack, would you please answer the phone?" But it had gone silent also.

The door again swung open, and three guns swung to meet..........May Mullally, daughter of Portuguese immigrants, and wife of Assemblyman John E. Mullally, saloon keeper. She screamed at the horrific scene that greeted her. "John, are you alright?" She embraced her husband, who was covered in blood and bits of bone, meat and brain tissue. Crenshaw stuck his gun in Mullally's waistband and slipped out the door as May explained she had seen the three men looking suspicious outside the saloon, and had tried to phone to warn him.

Tierney phoned the police as Mullally tried to clean himself off with his wife's help. The San Francisco police arrived faster than Tierney's call could allow, as the gunfire had caused many people to contact them.

The police investigation lasted for hours. One of their questions had to do with claims by several of the customers that there had been another customer present who had been the one to fire the first shots, as well as taking out the third bandit. But Assemblyman Mullally and bartender Tierney both denied the presence of another customer, now missing. The Assemblyman explained the initial non-fatal injuries in the man he had fought as coming from a Colt Sporting gun he was able to show them. His word was ultimately accepted, since the only surviving criminal was in no condition to discuss possible disappearing witnesses.

The saloon was closed for clean up on the Fifteenth, but as "Bates" had suggested, the day's newspapers were filled with the story. Mullally was profiled as the "Battling Assemblyman" who had heroically defeated the three nearly single-handedly.

The crooks were identified as soldiers, one from the Presidio, the others from other military bases around the Bay Area. A stream of people came by to view the scene and express opinions to Mullally. One of the first to appear was one of the three candidates Mullally had defeated to win his assembly seat. "Mr. Shelton, I certainly never expected to see a Prohibition Party candidate in my saloon."

"Oh, Mr. Mullally, I would hope this experience would inspire you to seek a higher calling than purveyor of demon rum."

"Actually we get little call for rum. Beer is the most popular, followed by whiskey."

"Yet even after this you still find nothing wrong with selling any of those."

"Apparently neither do the voters of the 30th Assembly District. Didn't I have nearly a hundred votes for every one you received?"

Shelton shook his head and turned to leave, with one last parting shot. "The Prohibition Party continues its work, and someday we shall end this curse on America."

Mullally, who had already glanced at the materials Crenshaw gave him, startled Shelton by saying, "You're absolutely right, you're less than ten years from imposing Prohibition on all of the USA, and a sad day it will be."

Democrat William Doell was Mullally's next defeated opponent to appear. He deplored the rising tide of crime under Republicans. Mullally responded that the Democrats would take over the White House after November so come back in two years and we can compare results. Meanwhile, he said, *this* Republican knows how to handle crime effectively.

Last to show up was the Socialist candidate, Robert Larkins, who felt crime was evidence of the corruption of capitalism, and could not understand why Mullally, who had begun his political career in 1907 as a delegate to the Union Labor Party convention, did not support socialism as the only feasible economic way to protect the working class. Mullally just laughed at him.

17

When Crenshaw had not appeared by noon on the Eighteenth Mullally finally realized he had no intention of showing up again, and presumably had already returned to his time.

Headline on the *San Francisco Call* newspaper, November 3, 1920:

HARDING AND MULLALLY LEAD REPUBLICAN ROMP
Below is an extract from an article in the same issue devoted to Mullally:

After just a single term as a Congressman, John Mullally succeeded in unseating one term Senator James Phelan. Mullally, with extensive support from women who only gained the vote with passage of the Nineteenth Amendment on August 26, got almost precisely 50% of the vote to Phelan's 39.8%. James Edwards of the Prohibition Party got 6.3%, although his effort seemed unnecessary with passage of the Eighteenth Amendment. The Socialist Party's attempt to capitalize on women now being able to vote by running Elvina Beals, only managed to get 4.0%.

Extract from Inaugural Speech of John E. Mullally, January 20, 1941

We must not neglect to thank Franklin Roosevelt for his herculean effort over the past eight years to deal with the economic crisis, and I am sure some of his reforms, such as Social Security and Unemployment Insurance, will be of major help to America's workers in the future. Workman's Compensation would have helped my father after he was disabled on the job, so despite some in Congress hoping I would support repeal, in fact were such a repeal to pass Congress, I will be delighted to veto it. I hope to move forward in working for the betterment of all Americans, while keeping a wary eye on the on-going wars in Europe and the Far East. I won't repeat the broken promise Woodrow Wilson made to keep us out of the war, but I will not seek to get involved, either............

The Oval Office, the White House, Washington DC, February 15, 1941:

"Dr. Goddard, Dr. Oppenheimer, I am grateful both of you found time to accept my invitation to meet here." President Mullally gestured to a table set with coffee, juices, and various foods.

Robert H. Goddard smiled. "An invitation from the President doesn't come every day. I would never miss the opportunity."

J. Robert Oppenheimer added, "And few politicians seem ever to want to meet and talk to physicists!"

"We have a problem coming up for which you two can be a major part of the solution. To cut it short, the United States will be dragged into this war before Christmas. Dr. Goddard, I want you to work on developing rockets suitable for use in the war, some from shoulder launchers that can destroy tanks and similar armored targets, as well as long range rockets that can deliver bombs. Dr. Oppenheimer, you are to head the effort to develop the uranium or plutonium bomb."

Goddard gulped. "I've been ordered to stop testing in the Worcester area."

"Certainly, and I have to agree it was a dumb place to do tests. Stick with your wife's property in New Mexico."

"I'm flattered, " Oppenheimer began, "but surely Einstein is the most qualified."

"He's also way too high profile. Were he to leave Princeton for any reason, Hitler and Tojo would both suspect why. You may slip under their scrutiny, and can get other physicists, such as Dunning from Columbia, to work with you."

19

"Dunning? Sounds like you've been advised or done research on your own."

"Secrecy must be preserved. You will need uranium, and there just happens to be over 1300 tons of high grade uranium ore sitting in drums on the Staten Island waterfront. It came straight from the Belgian Congo after the Nazis overran Belgium. I suggest you try centrifuges as easier to handle than gaseous diffusion to separate the U235 isotope. I've already slipped in funding for both of you in the supplemental budget I added to what Roosevelt had submitted."

The Oval Office, the White House, Washington DC, April 27, 1941

President Mullally called in his secretary. "My nephew Bill died yesterday. Prepare a letter of sympathy on White House stationery to his widow for my signature. You can get her particulars in the family file. Start the letter 'Dear Jimmy'".

"Jimmy?"

"It's what the family calls her. Say a few words about the value of his contributions as a soldier in the last war, and as secretary of the San Francisco water commission. At the end say that we are likely to be dragged into the current war before Christmas, so don't be in a rush to sell the house and move Back East to join your family, because the prices of housing stock will zoom once we're at war."

"Oh, Mr. President, I hope you're wrong about the war."

"So do I, but it looks like a certainty. He had a kid, but at two years old I don't think a letter would mean much. Pick up a teddy bear at lunch, and have the mail room ship it."

The Oval Office, the White House, Washington DC, November 18, 1941

"Admiral Kimmel, General MacArthur, I'm very pleased you were able to leave your posts and join me for this conference."

Kimmel murmured some words about being honored by the invitation, while MacArthur scowled and said "As a military officer I always obey orders from my superiors."

"Unfortunately, this conference must deal with a very unpleasant subject. On Sunday, December 7, at about 7:45 am local time, a Japanese fleet will launch hundreds of bombers from the sea northeast of Hawaii, and attack our naval and land facilities. This fleet is commanded by Admiral Yamamoto, and has at least six large aircraft carriers and several battleships. There will be one or two man mini-submarines also attacking the harbor. Nine hours later Japanese ships and aircraft will attack Luzon while landing tens of thousands of troops there."

Both officers were horrified. MacArthur said, "How certain is this intelligence? I know I haven't heard anything hinting at this. Anyway, I doubt the Japs have the equipment or man-power to do all this while they're fighting China and the British." He looked at Kimmel, who shook his head.

"It comes from an unimpeachable source that has provided invariably correct intelligence in the past."

MacArthur started to argue, but Mullally cut him off. "Admiral, you will move all your ships out of the harbor under total radio silence starting not earlier than 2 nor later than 4 am on December 7. They are to head northeast, and assault the Japanese fleet from their flank. American aircraft are to fly at a high altitude, and meet the in-coming Japanese bombers at least fifty miles from land. I realize our radars are still primitive, but they should be sufficient to keep our units aware of the locations of the enemy."

Turning to MacArthur, he said "You are to assure all military aircraft in the Philippines are either in the air or hidden where bombing raids won't destroy them. I'm not sure where in Luzon the landings will take place, but have mines laid, artillery in place, and troops ready to shift as quickly as possible to resist. In the limited time left, try to bring the troops into a better state of preparedness to fight." He added, "And that goes double for you, Admiral. I realize you inherited a rather unprepared command. Do your best to improve it."

The two officers left the Oval Office. MacArthur said to Kimmel, "What do you intend to do?"

"Follow orders, of course. I'll need General Short's co-operation for the preparedness, and we'll try to practice at least twice moving all the ships out. I had been keeping them in port as easier to protect from sabotage, but the President doesn't seem to think that's a problem, at least not compared to the attack he described. He seems to have no faith in the talks Secretary of State Willkie has been having with the Japanese."

"I want to check with Hoover about this intelligence before I travel all the way back to Manila."

J. Edgar Hoover was ready to make time for an unscheduled appointment with Douglas MacArthur. "What brings you all the way from the far side of the world, General? Just to see me?"

"I just came from the White House, where the President informed Admiral Kimmel and me that the Japs are going to attack Pearl Harbor and The Philippines on December 7. Neither Army Intelligence nor Naval Intelligence knows anything about this. Do you?"

"Not a thing, and I do keep an eye on the Japs, the Nazis, and the Russkies. Did he say where this came from?"

"Just that it came from an 'unimpeachable source' that had never been wrong in the past."

"Such infallibility is only claimed for the Pope. What do you intend to do?"

MacArthur snorted. "I asked Kimmel the same question, and I guess I'll have to give you the same answer he gave me: follow orders. If nothing comes of this at least my men will get some needed training."

"I intend to follow up on this, and I'll let you know what I learn."

Hoover was fitted into the President's schedule two days later. "Mr. President, I understand you have unimpeachable intelligence of an impending Japanese attack. May I ask the source?"

"You may ask, but it's so secret that only the President can know the source, and I have to burn the writings after reading."

"I hope it's not a fortune teller or astrologer reading the stars, but some real spy."

Mullally forced a laugh. "No fortune tellers or mystic seers, I assure you. I wish it were, because I could ignore them. This comes from a far more unlikely, but much more trustworthy source."

"So you won't share this source with me?"

"I can't."

Hoover stomped away from the President towards the door. Mullally hesitated, thinking to himself that provoking Hoover was a fool's game, and he should be ashamed of himself for doing so. But as Hoover reached the threshold of the Oval Office, Mullally said, "By the way, you should advise the MI5 liaison that Kim Philby is a Soviet spy. So is Julius Rosenberg." Hoover visibly twitched, but did not stop or say anything.

~~~

2087, CRENSHAW RETURNS

Crenshaw looked around, puzzled. He seemed to be in a corridor of an office building. Several doors on each side, but nothing to suggest a Timely Adventures reception area. A woman coming down the hall looked fairly unremarkable. He said, "Excuse me, but I seem to have taken a wrong turn. Would you know where the reception area is for Timely Adventures?"

She stopped, and seemed to think for moment. "Sorry, but I don't know any firm by that name. Are you sure it's in this building?"

"I'm not sure of anything at this point." *Never heard* of Timely Adventures?! With all the advertising they do!

She pulled out a cell phone and typed something in. "Directory shows nothing by that name. What is it, a travel agency?"

"I thought so. Guess I'll go home and check the advertising brochure I received. Probably misread something; anyhow, thanks for your help."

"No problem." She continued down the hall. He headed for a marked exit. Outside two police, a man and a woman, were waiting.

"Sir, we had a complaint that a suspicious looking man was wandering this building. Would you mind identifying yourself?"

"I'm Herbert Crenshaw. I think I'm lost, because I was supposed to be met by representatives of Timely Adventures, and I can't find them."

"Have you any ID on you?"

"No, they were supposed to have my things—clothing, ID, whatever."

"Please stand still while I frisk you." Crenshaw couldn't decide whether to be outraged or frightened, but concluded he was in no position to resist. At least these cops seemed a lot more polite than he was accustomed to. The cop found the wallet he had carried in 1912, and opened it.

"This is curious. No ID of any kind, no credit cards, but a couple hundred dollars in extremely obsolete currency. Would you care to explain where you got this, and what the purpose is in carrying it around? You couldn't possibly expect any store to accept it."

"I just returned from 1912. I was there on an excursion set up by Timely Adventures, and I'm looking for their office so I can get a refund on the unspent cash, turn in these clothes, and get my own stuff back."

The cops looked at one another. The female cop said, "You wouldn't be playing games with us, would you?"

"Games? Why would I?"

The other cop nodded. "My handheld lie detector indicates you believe you were truthful although a bit evasive. Helping you is beyond our level, but Lt. Chen back at the precinct specializes in helping people with your sort of problem. Would you like to speak with him? It would be completely voluntary. You're not under arrest or any sort of restraint, but I think the Lieutenant could help. If it would make you feel better, you can ride in the front seat with me, rather in the back seat cage."

Crenshaw breathed a deep sigh of relief, and looked at the woman cop. "Would you mind being stuck in the back?"

"Not at all, " she said soothingly. "You ride up front like an innocent civilian. I'll be fine in back."

They all got into the patrol car with Crenshaw holding his suitcase on his lap. As the car started the male cop took a microphone, clicked a couple times, and said "Dispatch, this is Car 94. We have a probable 1074 coming in to see Lt. Chen."

"Acknowledge probable 1074. Lt. Chen will be notified."

At the stationhouse a police sergeant checked the contents of Crenshaw's suitcase, and asked him to leave it at the front desk. "Regulations prohibit civilians from carrying packages into the station. Don't worry, we rarely have burglaries here, so it'll be safe until you're ready to pick it up."

"I'm sure that's a joke about having burglaries here. Actually I'll be glad to leave the thing here, I'm tired of carrying it around."

The desk officer told them Lt. Chen was waiting in Conference Room 2, and after dropping their civilian off, they should get back to work. Both said they would first make a pit stop. Crenshaw went into Conference Room 2, and was mildly surprised to see Lt. Chen appeared to have African, not Oriental, ancestry.

"Good afternoon, sir. I'm Lt. Chen, but that's so formal. You can call me Paul. What might be your name?"

"Herbert Crenshaw."

"So Herbert, what's the problem that brought you here today?"

"I'm a customer of Timely Adventures. I spent three weeks back in the San Francisco of 1912, and expected when I returned to 2087 to be in their San Francisco reception center. So far no seems to know where that is."

Chen had been watching a panel on his desk not visible to Crenshaw. Chen looked up and said, "That's very interesting. What did you do in 1912?"

"Drink a lot of beer, party and carouse. I hope you don't think I tried to mess with the timeline."

"Why wouldn't you want me to think that?"

"I'm sure you're as acquainted as I am with the federal laws that can range all the way up to a death penalty for deliberately

25

messing with the past. Really, I hung out in a couple saloons, went to a show, picked up a couple ladies of what they called easy virtue, although to be honest, they probably hadn't had anything that might be called virtue since they were thirteen."

"Well!" Chen paused for a moment. "You needn't worry about federal laws, California's been a state for over 200 years, and we enforce our own laws, and let the feds do theirs. Tell me, when were you born?"

"August 24, 2054 in New York."

"Do you still live in New York?"

"Forty First Avenue in Flushing." On a sudden impulse he added, "That's the 108 Precinct."

"Excuse me for a moment." Chen worked a keyboard on his desk, then picked up a phone. Crenshaw could only hear Chen's end of the conversation. "This is Lt. Paul Chen of the San Francisco Police, " followed by a long and complex code he could not follow. "I have Herbert Crenshaw, a probable 1074, here who claims to have lived on 41st Avenue in your precinct." He looked at Crenshaw, and said "Exact address?"

He gave an address, and added "Apartment 9B."

Chen repeated this and asked for verification. A pause, and then "Thank you." A few more remarks, and he hung up.

"So, Herbert, I hate to disappoint you, but I can't help you any further. City and state law limit how much the police can do before turning problems such as yours over to licensed professionals. I do hope you are willing to see one. I have a civilian colleague who may be able to help. If you're willing, I can set up an appointment right now."

"If it will settle this nonsense, fine, do it."

Chen worked his keyboard. It spat out a sheet of paper. "We're in luck, Dr. Wollney can see you in a couple hours. I'll arrange a ride for you."

"What did the precinct say?"

"The address you gave me has been a supermarket for at least twenty years, and the precinct has no records of you."

"Oh, God, I've totally screwed the timeline! They'll hang me for sure!"

"So you feel a few beers and some time with ladies of the evening are so sinful you deserve to die? Should I tell Dr. Wollney how guilt ridden and depressed you feel?"

Crenshaw suddenly realized his best course was to shut up. Curiosity drove him to say, "Did you ever hear of John Mullally?"

"You mean President Mullally? His presidential library and museum is only a few blocks from here on Eighth Street."

"That's where his saloon was."

"And still is. The saloon survived Prohibition as a speakeasy, and got incorporated into the museum. Here's Patrolman Ghirardelli. He'll drive you to Dr. Wollney's office." He stood, and as Crenshaw rose with him, shook Crenshaw's hand. "Good luck. I respect Dr. Wollney's abilities, and hope she can help you."

As he passed the desk the sergeant handed Crenshaw his suitcase. He was about to say it contained nothing he wanted to keep, but decided the less said the better.

The drive turned out to be only a few blocks he could easily have walked, but Ghirardelli accompanied him into another office building, to a door labelled "Dr. F. Wollney, M.D., D. Psych., Fellow A.P.A., Diplomate AIPaC".

A receptionist signed a form Ghirardelli handed her. On retrieving it he nodded to Crenshaw, said "Good luck", and left.

The receptionist said to Crenshaw, "You were scheduled at the last moment, so you're at the end of the day. Would you want to sit here waiting for nearly three hours, or have you anything you might want to do for a couple hours?"

Crenshaw thought for a moment. "If it would be alright with you for me to leave this suitcase here, I think I'd like to visit the Mullally Museum."

She sighed. "Just put it over in the corner under the window."

He dropped the suitcase as instructed, said "I'll be back soon" and headed for the museum. Standing outside Crenshaw had a choice. Enter the saloon, or the main building of the museum and library. No choice at all. He had last been in the saloon three days ago of his time, 175 years for the saloon. It had surprisingly few changes. The back still had a bar, with shelves of liquor bottles, mugs and glasses above it. Broken glass and blood from the gun fight had been cleaned up. To one side was the mural of a god, still holding out a wine glass, still surrounded by maidens, although their gowns seemed less transparent than he had last seen them. The largest change was in the "free lunch" display. Cases were modern, a sneeze guard added. Mounted above, behind a clear covering, was what appeared to be his 1902 Colt. Looking closely on the opposite wall, he saw the bullet hole created when the third robber had fired at him was still there.

A woman wearing a sort of uniform with the word "Docent" on her left shoulder, said "Welcome to Mullally's saloon. Have you ever visited here before?"

Crenshaw smothered a laugh. "Yes, quite a few years ago. I was interested in how well you've preserved the place. I even see at least one of the bullet holes from the gun fight. I guess Mullally himself had all the broken glass and blood cleaned up."

"I fear broken glass would be dangerous for our visitors. You have sharp eyes to spot that bullet hole. It's not one we normally point out."

He raised an eyebrow. "Aren't all bullet holes created equal?"

"This one is hard to explain. The robbers were mostly firing at the bartender. So far as we know, nobody was in this corner."

"Didn't anyone ever say there was a customer sitting here who started the shooting?"

"Oh, you must be referring to the rumor of a sixth customer present who opened fire first. President Mullally always denied the sixth customer claim, and his bartender backed him up. There was never any evidence of a sixth customer."

"Good for Jack Tierney, always agree with the boss."

"My goodness, you certainly seem to have studied this well, to know the name of the bartender."

He gave her his most charming grin. "I learned long ago how important it is to make friends with bartenders. Speaking of which, are the bottles back there just for display, or do you ever serve drinks?"

"The saloon functions as the lunch room of the museum and library. So none of the bottles on display really contain alcohol. Most of our activity involves visiting school groups, and alcohol would be inappropriate. We do offer school children invented drinks that sound like something an old time saloon might serve, but it's just regular milk or other age appropriate drinks. There's an historical re-enacting group that comes here in the evening on the anniversary of the gun fight, and on that one occasion we do serve alcoholic beverages. Actually, we don't, the re-enactor portraying Jack Tierney does the serving."

"So no free lunch these days."

She smiled at him. "I fear that practice is long gone."

"Still, a shot of 175 year old whiskey might be interesting enough to attract an adult crowd."

"It probably would, but we would need a state liquor license, plus city law has restrictions we couldn't meet."

A man entered the saloon. He was expensively dressed, late fifties, tall, balding. The docent said, "Mr. Dressler, I've been waiting for you, and having a very interesting conversation with this gentleman, who seems exceptionally knowledgeable about President Mullally. Excuse me, " turning to Crenshaw, "but I never got your name."

"Herbert Crenshaw."

"Knowledgeable, eh? I'm planning a show on Mullally. Tell me something I don't know."

"I don't know about when he was in the White House, but when he was in the gun fight here he was a strawberry blond. If that's not good enough, a customer named Gilroy picked up the gun dropped by the third crook and used it to blow out the brains of the chief honcho, even though the press the next day made it sound like Mullally did most of the shooting. I don't think Tierney's gunfire accomplished much beyond distracting the crooks." He pointed to the gun on the wall. "If that's the original gun used in 1912, it only fired five times. Have the other two bullets been left in the magazine or were they removed?"

"Not bad, not that I necessarily believe it. Where did you learn all this?"

Crenshaw took a deep breath. "I was there."

The docent looked startled, and then giggled, assuming he was joking.

Dressler said, "You're pretty spry for someone over 200 years old."

"I'm 33. I'm a time traveler."

"And you went back to 1912 just to watch the gun fight that made Mullally famous?"

"No, I went back to save his life, because in the original timeline he was killed by the three robbers."

"Uh huh, and who won his Senate seat?"

"No one important. Franklin Roosevelt won the 1940 Presidential election."

"A third term? Nonsense, Roosevelt announced in April of 1940 he was retiring. He didn't mention it, but he was a cripple."

"In the original timeline he was afraid Dewey would be the Republican candidate, and Dewey was so opposed to much of Roosevelt's program that he decided to run. Dewey wanted to end support for England in the war, end Social Security, all sorts of stuff."

"Well, the war was over when Mullally died and Dewey inherited the Presidency, so he couldn't mess with Lendlease, but I don't remember him trying to end Roosevelt's social programs."

The docent said, "Actually he tried, but Congress blocked him. If I remember, it was one of the policies that helped the Democratic candidate, Eisenhower, defeat him in 1948."

"You know, Herb, " Dressler said, "you got a great imagination. Like I said, I'm producing a show about Mullally. Now it seems to me a book describing a world where Mullally died in 1912 just might stir up extra interest in my show. Plus you could make a few bucks. How about you and me sit down and discuss the possibilities?"

*REPRINTED FROM THE BOOK REVIEW SECTION OF THE NEW
YORK TIMES JUNE 22, 2088*

"Timely Misadventure", 2088, 314 pages, Dressler Publishing,
author Herbert Crenshaw?

Genre: Science Fiction; subgenres Alternate History, Dystopia

Reviewer: Dennis Farquhar-Jones

Alternate history is a long established genre within science
fiction. Dystopias have been around even longer. This book
offers an alternate history in which the famous Gunfight at
Mullally's Saloon ended very differently, with Mullally dead and
the robbers walking off with $87. Since this effectively wiped
out his twenty years in the Senate and his time as President, we
have an alternate history. What this history entails makes this
also something of a dystopia.

The first problem is finding out who the real author of this
book may be. There is no record of anyone named Herbert Crenshaw more than fifteen months ago. SF writers tend to have a
lengthy history of attending conventions, writing short stories,
and in other ways leaving footprints. Crenshaw seems in contrast suddenly to have appeared out of nowhere. But the book is
grammatical, has good character development, in all formal ways
is well written, not at all amateurish or the work of a beginner.
Clearly we are dealing with an accomplished main stream author
writing under a pseudonym. Regretfully I must say he was wise
to use a pseudonym, as *Timely Misadventure* offers an absurd,
illogical, and generally poorly thought out alternate history. The
author should stick to whatever part of main stream publishing
he normally writes for, and leave SF to its fans.

Changes induced by Mullally's early demise first show up
with Franklin Roosevelt running for and winning a third term.
Supposedly he feared Dewey would win and reverse Roosevelt's
Lendlease program supporting Britain early in World War 2, and
repealing Social Security. But despite his support of Britain, in
this third term Roosevelt does nothing to beef up defenses in
Hawaii or The Philippines. Japan, which walked into an ambush

when it attacked Pearl Harbor, in this alternate history destroys America's Pacific fleet in the sneak attack. Why would Roosevelt have ignored the secret intelligence Mullally put to such effective use? And even though The Philippines were attacked nine hours after Hawaii, in this improbable history, General MacArthur has done nothing to prepare. Were he still alive, he should sue "Crenshaw" for portraying him as grossly incompetent.

The author gets too cute by having Roosevelt die in office the same month that Mullally did. Roosevelt is succeeded by an obscure Missouri senator even few historians could describe. He beats Dewey to win his own term in 1948. Actually of course, Dewey succeeded to the Presidency, but lost in 1948 to Democrat Eisenhower. "Crenshaw" has Eisenhower as the victorious *Republican* candidate in 1952. Again, far too cute.

What makes this something of a dystopia, however, lies in the international picture. Instead of Berlin, and Hitler, being destroyed by an atomic bomb in 1944, with Germany's military subsequently suing for peace, "Crenshaw" has Germany defeated in 1945 by the invading armies of the USA, Britain, and the Soviet Union, with the Soviets occupying half of Germany and all of eastern Europe. Japan *is* defeated by atomic bombs, but a good nine months after it really happened. The Soviets then begin a "Cold War", which in "Crenshaw's" terminology means constant hostility plus a series of minor wars in which American forces faced Soviet proxies. Tens of thousands of Americans die in these wars, and inflation brings the dollar's value crashing. American politics turn inward to the point where Presidents appoint the Senate and state Governors, and suppress critics. I give the author points for a dark vision, but with the nuclear tipped rockets Goddard and Oppenheimer developed late in the war, even Stalin had enough sense not to challenge American might.

So why is the space program in this benighted world a good fifty years behind us? An arbitrary idea?

In summary, I cannot recommend this book, and cannot understand why in just a month after release it is number two on the Times current best seller list.

This was first published in the October 30, 2017 issue of *Bewildering Stories*.

AN ARKHAM HALLOWEEN

Our town holds public events for all sorts of holidays, official or unofficial. Arbor Day sees tree plantings along roads and in parks, even school grounds. Official holidays such as the Fourth of July we go all out, the loudest and best celebration in the state. Halloween is mainly for children who don't know better, but one year events may have gotten out of hand.

Some of Arkham's older residents have always cautioned against tempting fate around Halloween, but most adults look with a benign eye on children dressing as ghosts, goblins, witches or wizards as they collect their Halloween candies or cookies to the chants of "Trick or Treat".

The stranger approached me as I headed down Main Street. "Pardon me, sir, I'm looking for the library at Miskatonic University."

"Straight ahead about four blocks is the entrance to their campus. But why the library?"

"It put out a call for help. They have the original draft of *The Necronomicon* in Abdul al Hazred's own handwriting, and are looking for help to prepare a modern English language edition. Since I knew h—, uh, know how to read Medieval Arabic, I've offered my services."

"Well, good luck with that. You'll have to wait a few days, because the university, like much of the rest of this town, closes down for Halloween observations."

"No problem, at my age I've learned patience, so I'll...ah... tarry awhile. Know any bed and breakfasts or hotels where I could stay?"

"My aunt has a B&B. What's your name?"

"Joseph Ahasver. Feel free to call me Joe."

I gave Joe directions to my aunt's place, and told him to say I had recommended him.

A few hours later Aunt Ethel called to thank me for sending her a customer. "I've got both rooms rented out for a few days. And the one you sent me seems a lot more normal than the other fellow."

"How so?"

"This strange one, saying his name is Val Tepes, knocked on my door just after sunset to say he wished a room for a couple days. Spoke with a weirdo accent. Said he would not need any meals, so I knocked a couple bucks off for him. Of course, your fellow did ask if his meals could be kosher. I said I'd try."

"How's Gloria doing?"

"She and Bill still aren't making me a grandmother." She ranted on about this and other family matters. I finally got rid of her. The next morning gave her and the rest of town something new to discuss when the town drunk, old man Gauthier, was found dead. Instead of the expected broken neck from a fall in a drunken stupor, the coroner said he had two small bite marks on his neck, and seemed to be nearly totally exsanguinated. The sort of reason why kids did their trick or treating before sunset.

The day after was the day before Halloween, and the day of an unusual crime. Lovecraft Memorial Hospital had a raid on its blood bank, but only the B positive blood was taken. An overnight orderly swore he saw something, perhaps a giant bat, fly in a window adjacent to the refrigerated section where the blood was kept. I ran into Joe Ahasver on the street headed for a diner, and to be friendly joined him for lunch.

"So, my aunt treating you right?"

Joe smiled. "She's very chatty. I know almost as much about your cousin Gloria as you must from growing up with her. Is it true she hasn't had kids because she fears losing the ability to cast spells?"

I sighed. "My family has a long history of madness. One of our ancestors murdered his landlord and fed the meat to an investigator looking for the landlord, then screamed he could hear the victim's heart still beating."

Joe's eyebrows raised. "I remember the case. Your relative, eh?"

"It looks as though you'll have another case to remember, although I'm happy to think my family isn't involved in the death of old man Gauthier or the theft from the hospital's blood bank."

Joe shook his head. "I've heard similar things in my travels. Not good, definitely not good."

Hours later things came to a head. My cell phone showed Aunt Ethel was calling me, but when I opened it all I could hear was a distant voice sounding like her screaming for help. I raced in the evening's gathering darkness to her house, passing Joe on the way. I called to him to help, and within minutes the two of us burst into her home. Feeble cries came from her sitting room. We found her sprawled across a sofa, Val holding her down. His open mouth betrayed enormous incisors he was lowering to her neck. I leaped at him. With a casual gesture he swept me away. My head struck a wall. Dazed, I lay there.

Dimly I heard Joe say, "So, Count, we meet again after so many years, this time in the New World."

"I've no interest in you, Jew. Let me feed, and I'll not harm you."

"Isn't feeding on your hostess is bit extreme, one might even say careless?"

"My favorite flavor is B positive, but it isn't all that common. This garrulous old woman has it, as did the drunk."

I think I moaned. Joe, however, took an icon from a pocket and thrust it at Val, who spat out something in a foreign language. He jumped at Joe, who met him with a dagger. My blurry vision suggested the hilt bore a six pointed star. Val snarled "I'm not one of your Semitic tribe. The Mogen David symbol won't stop me."

"Perhaps not, but the dagger is silver, and was dipped in holy water. Or have you converted to Hindu? I have a vial of cow's blood, if necessary."

Val snarled something in English so disgusting I refuse to quote it. The blow to my head must have scrambled my brain, for it appeared he faded from sight and was replaced by a giant bat, which smashed its way out a window.

It took a couple hours for Ethel and me to recover. She started complaining Val had left without paying. Joe said he would cover Val's charges, adding, "I'm bound to see him again some day, and he'll pay. Meanwhile, I'll stay in town until I can finish my work in the university's library."

I think I know who they claimed to be, but that's not really possible, is it?

MILITARY PRECEDENT?

"Dung spread it, Fwedd! I have enough problems with the Raqqs' counterattack in northern Kalifya, and reinforcing Kyuva without listening to your nonsense of paleontological silliness."

"But General, we may have a key to a human weapon beyond anything we or the Raqqs ever dreamt of."

"Humans? Tales for children. They vanished what? 35 million years ago? If they were so great, where are they? Maybe next you'll go back a hundred million years and send a tyrannosaur against the Raqqs? I hear trilobites were probably poisonous if you want to try 300 million years." His growl falsified any thought he might be trying to be funny.

"They may have killed themselves with this weapon."

"*May* have? You and your paleontologist fools should be shut down so we can use the resources they waste to crush the Raqqs. If the forces on Kalifya are defeated that means we've lost the best site for launching an invasion from the west of their continents. Which makes the invasion from Kyuva in the east a bit pointless. Next choice are those frozen islands in the north, and maybe you forgot, but Raqqs area lot better adapted to extreme cold than we are. Beside which, they hold those islands and may be planning to invade *us* from them."

General Kharg bared his teeth as he glared at a portrait of a Raqq warrior adorning a wall of his office. The sharp, pointy snout, the dark areas surrounding its eyes like a mask, gray fur, bulky body contrasted with Kharg and his people, who were slender, relatively flat face, brown with orange speckles on their fur, and unlike the Raqqs' fat appendage, a slim prehensile tail. The General turned back to the situation map. He had ships contesting the northern end of the strait separating Kalifya from the Raqqs' northern continent, but the Raqqs seemed to have an unlimited supply of naval support. He stood there muttering to himself. Those in the room could only understand his mutters when he loudly made scatological comments about Raqqs.

Fwedd took a chance, and said "This seems to have been a bomb that could destroy an entire city."

"Dung talk. More fables for children!" He hurled a sculpture of a banana from his desk at Fwedd, who ducked and ran from the room.

Fwedd's next move was to contact his paleontologist friend, Professor Nargyo. When informed of the General's reaction, Nargyo said, "Not surprising, but I have some contacts in the physical sciences back at the university where I teach. Let's see if one of them can help."

Nargyo's colleague was Professor Melpat, who wanted to know where this paleontological finding was located. "I don't mind a bit of travel, but your digs seem always to be in unpleasant, remote locations with a terrible climate. What's this one?"

Nargyo had a totally innocent expression as he said, "This dig is in a major city. I trust you won't mind staying in one of their better hotels?"

"Amazing. What city?"

"Qakh."

"But that's the Raqqs' capitol!"

Fwedd giggled as Nargyo shrugged. "The site's really on the shoreline of the island of Jibtanz."

Melpat scowled. "Now that you've had your little joke, what does this discovery look like?"

Nargyo presented a photo of an object which may, 35 million years ago, have been a long, sleek narrow body.

Melpat and Fwedd both exclaimed, "A submarine!"

"I think so also. Shape is often determined by use, and an underwater vehicle pretty much needs this shape."

"So how did it end up on Jibtanz?"

Nargyo took up a professorial stance as he lectured. "Our southern continent split not too many millions of years ago.

The loose piece, now the island of Jibtanz, is drifting eastward and northward. It kicked up a lot of ocean bottom, including what seems to have been this human submarine that today lies in some upraised ocean floor. The remains of human ships have been found all over the world, but this is the first one that is unquestionably military. I hope to find identifiable weapons."

Fwedd looked puzzled. "Continents can split? How?"

«We don't know all the details, but the Raqqs' southern continent and ours split from one another about 300 million years ago. Just compare the coastlines. In fact, it appears Kalifya split off their northern continent just a couple million years after humans went extinct, and has been drifting northwest ever since. More recently Jibtanz split from the east side of our southern continent."

"Assuming all this is true, " said Melpat, "I'm interested. How soon can we leave?"

Wartime travel was something of a hassle, but Fwedd used his influence as a staff officer in charge of supply, and within the month they found themselves at the only airport on Jibtanz. From there Nargyo took charge, taking them to a remote rocky outcropping on the eastern shoreline. As they traveled Nargyo said, "Our geologist colleagues recently discovered an oddity. All over the world there is a thin layer of an otherwise very rare element, iridium, right at the point where the dinosaurs disappeared. And right at the point where the humans vanished, a thin layer not of iridium, but of lead. But this isn't ordinary lead. This is 85 to 90 percent lead 207. Most naturally occurring lead has only 16 to 20 percent of the 207 isotope."

"Sounds like you and your geologist friends are invading my field, " Melpat said. "Any theories of why the lead should be odd?"

Nargyo looked puzzled. "I was just bringing Fwedd up to date. I'm sure you were consulted by the geologists about this."

"True enough, but I can't come up with a reasonable explanation for the isotopic imbalance. We do know that some isotopes of lead are the final stage of radioactive decay of uranium or other radioactive elements, but lead 207 is only the result of decay from a recently created artificial element, number 94. It's created when we hit uranium's most common isotope with helium ions."

"Artificial element?"

"It can't exist in nature, we create it, thus 'artificial'".

"Why can't it exist naturally?"

Melpat sighed. "I feel like I'm teaching introductory physics. It decays so fast half is gone in about 21, 000 years."

Nargyo said, "Then in 35 million years lots of lead 207 where this element 94 was!"

Fwedd tried to bring this back to his concern. "Could element 94 have been used in some sort of weapon?"

Nargyo waved his tail in doubt. Melpat looked thoughtful.

When they arrived at the shore front site they found workers engaged in removing rocks and dirt from around the supposed 35 million year old submarine, with a naval captain supervising. He walked over to the group and introduced himself. "I'm Captain Bwagharo of the Submarine Command. We hope to see if the humans knew anything about submarines that we could learn from."

The group's members introduced themselves. Melpat asked if any large deposits of lead had been found in or around the artifact. Bwagharo's tail perked up as he said, "Interesting you should ask. We found four lumps of lead. Two seem to have been in what may have been torpedoes. One looks a bit like the torpedoes, but it seems to be aimed straight up, which makes no sense. Why would a submarine go directly underneath an enemy ship to fire a torpedo? Anyhow, the last one seems to have been part of their power system, which I don't understand."

The new arrivals had no answers for either problem.

Nargyo then said, "Why would their torpedoes have used element 94? Does it make an explosive?"

Only Melpat looked as though he might have an answer, but did not speak.

The group watched the workers briefly, and then went to the headquarters Bwagharo had established in a temporary shack. The discussion centered on the presumptive vertical torpedo briefly. When that proved fruitless, they tried to figure out how this extinct element 94 could have served as both a weapon and a power source. Melpat finally said, "One of my colleagues back at the university has been trying to interest the government in experimenting with the possibility that 94 may in fact cause an explosion if a large enough mass is hit with neutrons. The atom would fission with an enormous release of energy. The lead in this human artifact suggests to me that they were using 94 as a powerful weapon."

Fwedd said, "As a supply officer my first thought is how do we get enough of 94 to make one of these weapons?"

Nargyo added, "What besides an enormous explosion might result? Why would the humans have made such explosions over every inch of the planet, because we find a thin layer of lead 207 everywhere."

Fwedd said, "We've had wars within our race. So have the Raqqs. No reason to assume the humans didn't also."

Melpat said, "I agree, especially with this lead 207 found everywhere."

Bhwagharo asked, "In addition to exploding, could this element 94 somehow be a power source?"

"It would be a source of heat, so I suppose you could figure out a way to harness that to power machinery—even, " Melpat added, "a submarine."

"But what about creating an explosion?"

"Look around us, " Melpat said. "We're out in this dung forsaken beach on a dung forsaken island. Do you see any of my technical materials or reference books? I need to get back to my office so I can research this. Little work has been done on element 94; it doesn't even have a proper name yet. Give me a few weeks of research and consultation with colleagues."

That pretty well squelched further discussion on element 94, lead 207, or potential mysterious explosives. Further investigation centered on the strange "vertical" torpedo, and the power source of the human submarine.

Melpat was not heard from for weeks after returning home, but finally contacted Fwedd. "I'll spare you the technical details, but it appears that a sufficient amount of element 94 can be made to explode in an enormous and violent process. I estimate an amount not weighing more than a small artillery shell could destroy an entire city the size of the Raqqs' capitol.....or of ours, for that matter."

Fwedd caught his breath in excitement. "Can we make enough of this artificial element to build such a bomb?"

"It would be expensive, but it can be done. But I have been consulting with geologists about that lead 207 layer. They suggest that in addition to the known meteor craters scattered around the world, there are also hundreds of mostly heavily eroded craters that have no obvious connection to meteors or to volcanoes. Their pattern suggests they were possibly formed all at the same time, and were made artificially."

"You mean the humans used some of these element 94 super bombs to make these craters?"

"That or something even worse."

Fwedd's excitement was unbounded as he contemplated bringing this news to General Kharg. "How soon do you think we could start making these super bombs?"

"Probably we could have useful weapons within three years of starting work. But we had best consider the danger. Humans seem to have used such bombs, based on the lead 207 layer, and look what happened to them."

A companion, not a sequel, to "Military Precedent?" Both have appeared in *Aphelion.*

REPEATING MISTAKES

The Raqq intelligence officer scowled. The information made little sense, and that meant he had to report it without being able to explain.

His commander took the report, and said, "How definite is this?"

"An economic journal mentions it, as do two different science publications, and there was a small note in a college alumni magazine."

"Food rot! I don't understand, but in wartime who knows what's important? I'll have to kick this upstairs. Someone in Qakh may understand."

The Raqq Intelligence headquarters had no idea how to interpret this oddity either, but called in several advisors. One said, "Uranium has several forms. Most are merely slightly radioactive..."

The Intelligence officer growled, "You think they plan spreading radioactive dust?"

"No, sir, uranium is not a good choice for that, and it would leave the land unusable for the monkhs also."

"So?"

"Theory suggests one form can be made into a super bomb. There's even a theory most of the craters on Earth happened because the humans used such a bomb on themselves."

"Whose theory? What evidence?"

"Ghornokh originated the theory. Should I have him brief you?"

The briefing went badly, as Ghornokh had problems speaking on a level most could understand. But enough got through.

The Raqq initiated a program to develop a superbomb based on uranium, just in case the monkh were doing the same, and might be successful.

This is the third and final story in the sequence of "Military Precedent" and "Repeating Mistakes". Apologies and thanks to David Brin for the title.

DOWNLIFT WAR

"Sir, we've received a demand for a peace conference."

"So the kazz are ready to surrender?"

"No, it's from the dolfsss."

"Dolfsss?!We learned they were intelligent centuries ago, but they've always ignored us."

"They seem to have changed their minds. Every ship we have at sea was approached with the demand. And they emphasized it by warning a mine sweeper to evacuate, and then sinking it."

"Son of an unwhelped bitch!"

"It appears they've also contacted the kazz."

"Did they deign to provide a time and place for this proposed conference?"

"Yes, noon, fifteen days from now off the east coast of Soam."

"Have we a choice? What if we refuse?"

"They threaten to sink every ship we have, naval or civilian, and destroy some bridges and tunnels. They claim the kazz got the same threat."

"Any indication of why the dolfsss finally are interested in what happens on land?"

"No, slr."

"May they chew meatless bones. Alright, have the staff prepare for leaving for this conference."

***

"We thank you for coming to this conference, and apologize for sinking one of your ships to emphasize our seriousness in inviting you."

"The ship is minor. You've always ignored us, except for a few legends about rescuing someone from drowning. We've fought wars in the past without your interference. Why not now?"

"Allow us to explain. You are aware of the fossils from fifty million years ago of humans?"

"Of course. What do they have to do with this?"

"Your scientists have found many craters dated to the same era as the human extinction. They have also found similar craters fifteen million years old coinciding with the extinction of the raqqs and monkhs. These are not coincidences. We dolfsss have records showing these extinctions came as a result of all these species wiping themselves out using superweapons. We would not care except that our records show that each time close to a third of our people died either from the weapons directly, or from fallout."

"What's fallout?"

"Trust me, you are better off not knowing. Regardless, we have decided not to allow this to happen a third time. We detected both you and the kazz are working to develop the superweapons. This we will not allow. You and the kazz will cease these developments, or we will intervene and prevent you from continuing your war. The choice is yours, the alternatives are proven extinction, our intervention, or peace."

Perhaps you need bit of physics to understand this.

FAVORED PET

Erwin Schroedinger took his favorite pet to his veterinarian for a check up. The vet left him in the waiting room, and took the pet in its carrier to an examination room. An hour later the vet came back and said, "Professor Schroedinger, I have good news and bad news about your cat."

THE NEED FOR SPELL CHECK

Father harrumphed, and said, "Well, we can be hysterical and fear the sky is falling."

Bruce looked up from some exceptionally dull math homework, hoping Father's notorious jokes were about to offer an interesting alternative to algebra. Mother seemed a bit nervous, having had a few experiences with his bad jokes. Father ended the anticipation by saying, "The Chinese messed up the launch of their new spaceship, Tien Chuen. It's barely reaching 350 kilometers at peak, and dipping back to 112. Reports say it'll crash somewhere over the USA next week instead of docking with their space station."

Mother shrugged. "Is there any chance it could land near here?"

"America's a big country, and right now the prediction is just about anywhere. But if you want to worry, our insurance specifically excludes coverage for falling spacecraft."

Bruce laughed. Then he sadly returned to his homework. After dinner he linked up with his best friend, as Richard came by. The two embraced, and kissed, their tongues engaging in a wrestling match that ended with the two sprawled on his bed. "So what's new and maybe exciting?"

Bruce described the wayward Chinese spacecraft. Richard listened and then said, "You think we could maybe influence where it crashes?"

"I don't know. Have you ever cast a spell on something in space?"

"Nope, never even thought of it. Hey, what if we could keep it from crashing?"

"I suspect that would break the rule that we aren't supposed to do anything that attracts attention or reveals our powers."

"So influencing where it crashes wouldn't attract attention?"

"Depends on how much we change its flight path. Stuff falling from space gets influenced by all sorts of things, like weather fronts and atmospheric pressure. Hey, I sound like the weather reporter on the evening news."

"Yeah, but you ain't as good looking!"

"Good enough for you." They pushed each other and had a brief mock wrestling match, highlighted by many improper holds below the belt. When this ended Bruce led the two of them to the secret den where his sorcerous materials were kept. The two spent half an hour rummaging through things to find what might be usable for a spell affecting a spacecraft. Their set up included a globe, a pair of chopsticks from a Chinese takeout to represent the Tien Chuen, a bird's feather, worn umbrella, and other useful material.

It being Bruce's collection, he pulled from a nearby shelf a book with the title"Al Azif" on the cover, and began crafting a spell to shift the spacecraft's orbit. Richard frowned at the choice of grimoire, but chimed in at appropriate moments. There was a sudden puff of smoke, releasing a disgusting odor. The chop sticks crumbled into ash, as did the feather. The umbrella lost a couple ribs. "Wow, that sure didn't work!"

"So what went wrong?"

"You got me. Maybe some of the stuff I was using was fake, or maybe we said the wrong thing."

"Fake chop sticks? Fake feather? Gimme a break. You're just too stupid to use Spell Check."

"But the chop sticks were supposed to be a stand in for a Chinese spacecraft. If they were made here, they were so wrong it could have caused the mess up we just saw."

Richard said, "Next time we use some of my stuff, and I *will* use Spell Check. Come over to my house after school tomorrow."

"No sweat. I'll tell my folks we're doing a homework problem together."

"Cool. See you tomorrow."

Richard had prepared a fancy set up in his attempt to influence the wayward Chinese spaceship. A standard globe stood on his desk. Near it was a scale model spacecraft purchased at the local hobby shop, which had no idea a major portion of its business depended on kids practicing magic. The other objects were designed to focus their psychic energies (or perhaps just their attention to their magic, neither being known for their focus on details).

Bruce looked at the set up and said, "Wow, I'm almost jealous."

"Don't be. I figured with what happened when we tried yesterday I should have some ideas on improving things. Look, we got this globe. I gonna hang the model spaceship by it, and then we got the incense. The Chinese gotta get the spaceship higher, so the incense and a bit of beer I 'borrowed' from my dad will make us high."

"We're stand ins for Chinese astronauts?"

"I read they call 'em taikonauts, but yeah."

"That's pretty dangerous being a stand in, and there's just two of us, but the news said they got five on board. You got any idea the effect of too few of us would be?"

"You got a better idea?"

"Sure, we invite some kids from school to be the stand ins, while we do the spell nice and safe. Our class at school got lotsa kids who would be interested enough to volunteer, especially if they hear they get some beer. I'll bet some of those kids would do anything for a beer."

"Cool, bro. I'll keep this stuff together until we can bring 'em here. Got any idea when?"

"Saturday after the game sound good to you?"

"Perfect. I'll tell the kids at school and my parents we're having a party after the game. Probably have volunteers showing up, so we can have stand ins for the taikonauts and the launch crew. More power and better spells."

Eight of their classmates showed up for the announced party. After checking the latest news coverage of the troubled spacecraft five were selected as stand ins for the taikonauts. The remaining three were moved to a corner of the party room, where they faced a computer console masquerading as launch command. Richard removed the table cloth he had hiding the globe and model spacecraft. One of the stand ins, Carl, said

"Hey man, what's that crap for? Looks like a school thing. You really need school crap at a party?"

Bruce said, "Relax, man, I need a couple of volunteers for a project. If you don't want to help, don't. I'm cool with it either way."

Richard added, "Yeah, and it kinda inspires me when I want to sing. Here, try the beer we liberated from my dad."

Several of the other kids told Carl to chill out, if Richard needed something for a school project, that didn't hurt the party.

Carl took a swig, and as his face crinkled, took two more deep swallows before he passed the bottle to another of the stand ins. Bruce lit the incense. Richard began chanting a spell.

Carl snickered, and a girl sitting at the computer console called out, "If that's the best you can do at singing, shut up!" Carl laughed so hard he almost fell off his chair. Bruce cautiously tied him back in with a simulated seat belt, figuring taikonauts probably used them anyway. Carl grabbed the bottle of beer while everyone's attention was diverted.

Richard kept the chant going. Bruce joined him in several spots. Jim, another guest who was an unknowing stand in for a Chinese astronaut, stared suspiciously. "That sounds like stuff we were warned against in church." He pulled a crucifix out of his shirt and waved it at the two party hosts.

Richard sneezed and coughed loudly, followed by collapsing into a nearby chair. Bruce nearly landed on the girl who had told Richard to shut up. The model spacecraft next to the globe fell to the floor. Steam issued from some of the other materials. The entire party dissolved into yelling and shouting, some at Jim, some at the hosts, and some at just about everyone else. Carl gradually fell silent, eventually sitting looking dazed from the drinks he had.

Bruce cursed loudly and with passion, describing Jim and his parents, grandparents, dog, and various random relatives in the most vulgar terms he was capable of. Jim turned to a couple of the other guests and suggested they all leave. With the mess on the floor and elsewhere, and Carl clearly out of it, the other guests left.

The two would be saviors of the spacecraft were left with a clean up, plus the problem of what to do with a drunken Carl. They completed the clean up still cursing Jim, and then turned to Carl. Richard said, "I've had some thoughts on a spell to counteract hangovers. Maybe a slight modification could make him sober."

"What sort of spell?"

"It breaks the chemical bonds in the alcohol molecule. You get water and carbon dioxide."

"Your chem is screwed up. Alcohol has two hydrogens and two oxygens with one carbon. Water and carbon dioxide would have the carbon and two hydrogens, but three oxygens."

"Well, listen to Mr. Einstein. Maybe it's carbon monoxide."

"Which is poisonous. You ain't thinking straight."

"So you want to leave him here drunk until he wakes up? How do I explain that to my parents? And his parents might get a little concerned when he doesn't come home."

"You got a point. But we can't try your spell if it produces carbon monoxide because it could kill him. Boy, we sure aren't getting anywhere with saving that spaceship, and we're down to three days before it crashes somewhere."

"Let's solve the Carl problem first." Richard went to his computer and made a search on how to get rid of alcohol. "Here we are, the body gets rid of alcohol by having the liver metabolize it. I'll cast a spell to make his liver work extra fast."

"Is that safe?"

"It's got to be safer than having any of our parents find him drunk."

Bruce shrugged. "I guess so. Can I help?"

"We have to figure out a spell that works on his liver. Got any ideas?"

"Yeah, but I need a liver to work on."

"I'll see if we got any in the fridge."

A few minutes later Richard showed up holding something wrapped in refrigerator paper. "Here's some chicken liver. Will that do for whatever you're planning?"

"We'll see." Bruce took the liver, handing back the other giblets. Richard hesitated, looked like he might throw them out, and then returned to the kitchen. Bruce completed preparations, including rubbing the chicken liver on Carl, thus invoking both the law of similarity and the law of contagion. Fully charged with magical influences, he commanded Carl's liver to break down the alcohol quickly.

By the time Richard had returned, Carl was awake, looking slightly dazed. They helped him out to the porch, where he sat for a short while before staggering home.

"Look, " Richard said, "we've been going about this badly organized. You started with a fake similarity with those American origin chopsticks. We've no possibility for using the law of contagion. I was looking at my class notes, and I think we might do best with metonymy."

"That's stuff we won't cover until next semester. You been reading ahead?"

"Of course. Don't you?"

"I have enough trouble keeping my grades up in history and math, damn it."

"Well, I've read some on it, and I think we should give it a try."

"Is it even still worth it? It's supposed to come down in three days, and I'm sure NASA and the Chinese are trying to come it with a rescue plan."

"Nuts with NASA, they can't even launch people into space these days. And it's the Chinese who created the problem. Maybe if Russia weren't so busy invading places."

"Yeah, sure. So you're so great, show me what you can do with metonymy."

Richard pulled out a science textbook, and opened to a photo of the Moon. He began a strange chant in which the Chinese Tien Chuen was described as the Moon's younger brother, continuing to urge younger brother to grow up and ascend to his proper place. The Chinese goddess Chang'e was invoked for her help. Bruce caught the rhythm and joined in, lighting some incense as he chanted. The procedure lasted nearly an hour before both were close to collapse from exhaustion.

"So, " Bruce gasped, "did it work?"

"Turn on the news."

They found CNN, where a reporter was saying, "The Chinese spacecraft that has been threatening to fall back to Earth in a couple days seems to have managed to restore power to its thrusters, and is now in a circular orbit nearly 400 kilometers up. It should easily stay in orbit long enough for a proper rescue mission, and may even be able to reach their space station for an emergency docking."

REPORT TO THE COLONIZATION OFFICE

Planet: 48229-3

Atmosphere: pro—oxygen adequate; **con**—high level of pollutants, increasing CO_2 levels affecting climate

Axis Tilt: 0.409 radian

Density: 5.52

Diameter: 6143 ggord

Land/water ratio: 29/71

Orbit: *semimajor axis*—88, 520, 269 ggord
      eccentricity—0.01671
      period—412 lfibb; 365.2422 p.d.

Rotation: 19.77 hrida

Surface gravity: 10.11

Weather: temperature range acceptable, surface subject to violent weather due to local sapients damage to atmosphere

Biota:
vegetation—extensive, diverse, incompatible for food
animals—many on land and sea. Few dangerous
sapients—numerous and possessing nuclear weapons

RECOMMENDATION: Not suitable until local sapients have exterminated themselves

Life need not always be pure science fiction. This may be a bit more impure than most.

FOR SALE

As Mike sat guzzling a beer, a stranger said, "You look new. What brings you to Brady's Bar?"

Mike almost didn't bother to respond, but finally he sighed, and said, "The bastards at the Board of Health closed my favorite bar, so I'm left drinking in this dive." He demonstrated his point with a deep draft.

"You seem sort of depressed."

"Yeah, my company just filed for bankruptcy, so I'm out of a job. But the friggin' CEO got a five mill golden parachute. Plus I got a notice the city's street widening scheme means they take 1.95 meters off the front of my house. My daughter just ran off with her boy friend. He's with some damn punk heavy metal band called the Purple Electric Eel, and he's not even a musician, just one of their roadies. My son's in Afghanistan studying Shari'a at a madrassa, and my wife gave me a dose of clap before running off with the milkman. Depressed? Nah. I'm friggin' dancing for joy."

"Maybe this call could help you." The stranger handed him a card. It bore nothing but an 800 number.

"What's this crap?"

"I'm what you might call a recruiter. Our firm helps people with problems."

"For a price. Except I'm out of work and can't afford nothin'."

"Can you afford a phone call to an 800 number? That obligates you to nothing."

Mike shrugged and stuck the card in a pocket. He had another beer before heading home. He had almost forgotten the incident in the bar until coming across the card as he prepared for bed. After hesitating he picked up the phone and dialed.

"Welcome to Hellfire and Damnation. If you know the extension of your demon, you may dial it at any time. For information on a coven near you, dial one. For curses, hexes and spells, dial two. For jobs with organized crime or the government, dial three. For CFOs and CEOs of financial institutions or polluting industries, dial four. For fallen clergy or clergy who wish to fall, dial five. For all other occupations, dial six. For incubi or succubi, dial seven. To sell a soul, dial eight. To hear this menu again, press the star key."

Mike stared at the phone. Then he slammed it down. After a long pause he punched redial. After hearing the menu a second time, he hit two. "Thank you for dialing for curses, hexes and spells. All our demons are speaking with other clients, but please remain on the line for the next available demon. Your soul is important to us." Music played. Mike recognized an opera from a period when his daughter had been into classical music.. . Berlioz, he realized, *The Damnation of Faust.*

Finally a smooth, almost unctuous voice said, "Curses, hexes and spells. This is demon Brigu, who do you wish to be afflicted?"

"No, I want find out if *I*'ve been cursed."

"Ah, wrong office. Shall I transfer you?"

"Yes, please do." *(Hell seems as bureaucratic as any government agency.)*

Buzzes and clicks. Then in a voice that was almost snarl, "Office of Complaints and Minor Affairs. What's your problem?"

"I'd like to know if I've been cursed. I'm ...."

"We know who you are, wimp. You weren't cursed until you called here. Now you are."

GOOD FOR WHAT AILS YOU

Pelagic Hypertropism is a tragically uncomfortable disease whose occurrence is increasing. Your doctor may encourage you to try new, improved Mefystofilaze to alleviate the symptoms.

Mefystofilaze comes in a soft capsule filled with a gentle goo, guaranteed not to scratch the inside lining of your throat on the way down.

Mefystofilaze has not been used in comparative studies, so its advantages over alternative medicines, if any, are unknown. If symptoms persist, triple the dose.

If your blood type is AB positive or O negative, speak to your hematologist before using Mefystofilaze.

Use if you brushed your teeth in the past seven days is contraindicated. Use for more than 24 hours may cause 500 percent increase in ear wax production. Do not take if symptoms persist. If toilet paper sticks to you, see your doctor immediately. You should not take Mefystofilaze if you or your partner are pregnant or trying to get pregnant, as nauseating mutants can be produced. Not for use within five years after an appendectomy.

Abnormal skin lesions may appear. This is a normal physiological reaction, and is quite harmless, so if they do appear this is no cause for alarm. Uncontrollable bleeding may briefly occur. If elbows swell, take your favorite painkiller. Eyebrows should grow back within two months.

If breathing is hindered by excessive growth of nasal hairs, consult your barber.

In a small percentage of users intestinal upset has resulted in generating toxic gases that have rendered by-standers unconscious. Some patients have found themselves unable to breathe in the atmosphere when taking Mefystofilaze.

Dehydration may cause excessive loss of water, leading to increased thirst.

No one under the age of 35 should take this medicine, as its use by those younger than this has not been studied. Not recommended for anyone over the age of fifty or who has had a tonsillectomy. At least fifty percent of users of Mefystofilaze remain alive for at least two weeks after taking this medicine.

You should advise your airline if you will be traveling by air after taking Mefystofilaze. Do not drive or operate heavy machinery if you have taken this drug within one month.

The recommended dose of Mefystofilaze contains the following amounts of Recommended Daily Allowance:

uranium	27%
arsenic	21%
congealed fat	19%
mold	16.2%
butyl mercaptan	13.1%

Originally published in *Aphelion*. You probably have to be of a certain age to appreciate this.

RETURNING HOME

Ellis thought his track jumper had returned him to his home universe. Then he found out the first person on the Moon was Alice Kramden.

FAREWELL TO PRADANG

"Siddathamon Priddikachorn."

The person summoned glanced at his fellow supplicants, and decided wisdom advised he not speak loudly. "Why in bloody space can't these dumb off worlders teach their AIs to pronounce names correctly?" No one overheard him, so there was no reply, not that he would have expected one anyway. More likely he would have been reported by someone viewing him as a competitor to be eliminated. He rose and headed for the next available interview room.

A woman younger than he had expected sat at a desk. She waved him to the only empty chair in the room.

"Your academic record is sufficient to gain you admission to the University. Now we hope to learn more about you before deciding on actual admission. Is Pradang your home world?"

"Yes."

"So why do you want to leave it?"

"I'm interested in xenopaleontology, and none of Pradang's universities even offer a course in the subject. They're good for training people in our agricultural, cultural, and industrial needs, not much else."

"So, Mr. Priddikachorn...." His wince made her pause. "Is something wrong?"

"I may be too sensitive, but you mangled the pronunciation of my family name."

"I beg your pardon, but on my home world we have much simpler names." She stared at him for a moment. "Would you mind if I simplified your name to 'Pretty' while we are talking?"

He gave her a slight leer, and said, "Now that would be far more appropriate for me to call you."

She laughed. "Flirting with your admissions officer is a non-traditional means of gaining admission to the University. Let's stick to the topic. You are aware that Pradang's government tends to disapprove of people emigrating?"

"I don't want to emigrate, just get an education in my chosen field." She was no longer looking at him, but studying a panel invisible to him on her desk.

"So, Pretty, have you any additional motives such as an unhappy love affair?" She paused while he vigorously indicated a negative. His affairs were all light hearted and mutually temporary. "Or escape from debts?" again a negative. He didn't mention that by Pradang's standards his family was significantly more wealthy than the planetary average. "Politics?" He wasn't even polite in denying that one. Pradang was famous for its political apathy. Even though voters were rewarded with a week's pay when they voted, turnout rarely reached 35% of eligible voters even for important elections. "Use of substances banned on Pradang?" His response was almost contemptuous, which may have been reasonable considering how few substances Pradang banned.

"What would be your plans after completing a degree at the University?"

"I would hope to get a chance to do some field work on a few planets. Perhaps someday convince one of our universities to offer courses in xenopaleontology that I could teach."

After a few more inconsequential questions dealing with his finances and health, he was told that he would be informed if the University would accept him. Pradang's government had already approved his application to be allowed to study off world, so he returned home to await the expected good news, and to prepare to leave. He figured applying for a field that was not overwhelmed with competing applicants gave him an excellent chance at acceptance.

Four days later his complink, and those of his parents, brought the expected news. "Son, we're proud of you, " his Father announced, while holding out what was obviously an indent on a bank. Siddathamon, who was already thinking of himself as "Pretty", took the offering. An enormous sum, but not from his parents. It came from his *tailung*, or mother's elder brother, a distinction made on Pradang and a few other worlds. "Your *Tailung* Bardavong sent this to help you live on while you complete the degree. I trust you will properly thank him, and keep him apprised of your progress."

"That will be a pleasure, especially with this much money. What ever inspired him to give me so much? We've never been that close."

Mother answered, "Bardavong has no children, and he always was sort of my protector when we were growing up. I guess he feels he's passing that along to you."

Siddathamon's two younger siblings immediately demanded to know if Bardavong would give them as much money when they started college. Mother told them not to be greedy, and to let Bardavong decide for himself what was done with his money.

"May the gods reward and guard all such *tailung*. I shall see him before leaving in order to properly thank him." He took another look at the gift, and said, "This is in Federation money, not our local currency. That makes this even more enormous. Why not just in Pradang's money?"

"Pradang's money would have little value off world, especially someplace as far off as the University. Federation money is good anywhere."

"I guess so. By the way, the University's interviewer recommended that I use a simplified pronunciation of my name off world."

Father frowned. "We have an honorable name that goes back centuries to Earth. Why would you change it?"

"Not change, Father. Just a short version for off worlders who have trouble pronouncing it."

"And just what would you use for a short version?" Father was scowling, and even Mother looked distressed. His younger brother whispered something to their sister, who laughed.

"I was thinking 'Pretty' derives easily from Priddikachorn for those who are — mm — linguistically inept."

Father laughed loudly, and even mother smiled. "That should make them sorry they didn't try harder, and really confuse any off worlder who's ever seen your face." He kept laughing long enough for his son to start to feel a bit insulted. The younger members of the family jibed alternative names which were notable for the lack of dignity they implied. Mother smiled while trying to stop these alternatives.

The next few days were taken up with the usual details in leaving one world for another, and in heading for a new school. The local news media apparently was tipped off that a local boy was accepted to the galaxy's most prominent University, because Siddathamon found himself being interviewed, publicly displayed, and receiving congratulations from neighbors and teachers at his old school. Even some classmates, most of whom were not even jealous, contacted him. But he made time to visit his *tailung* in order to thank him properly.

The meeting took place in the *tailung's* private home, in an interior room Siddathamon had never seen before. Several devices around the room seemed designed to defeat recording or spy gadgets. Bardavong smiled at his *lungee*. "So, Siddathamon, you alone of all our world's graduates this year will carry your family name to the great University planet. Are you still dedicated to the study of alien fossils?"

"Yes, *Tailung* Bardavong. It is still my great interest."

"I suppose that this will at some point require you to visit many strange worlds, perhaps even some that humans have not been able to colonize, to study these fossils?"

"Indeed, and your most generous gift should make that much more easily possible."

"Hmm. And have you ever heard of an alien plant called dilbar?"

Pretty paused for a moment, and then said, "I seem to remember from taking biology that it has some medicinal uses."

"Just so. It is quite valuable because the source is unknown. Three worlds, unfortunately not including our beloved Pradang, import it from a distant unaffliliated world, location unknown.

There is a report recently that some seeds have become available, and several companies are seeking to grow them, so far without much success. I'm confident they can soon overcome whatever difficulties exist, but Pradang will not benefit by changing who profits from the limited source for dilbar. I would hope that when you go out seeking alien fossils you would also be alert to the possibility of identifying the source of dilbar and the reason for the difficulty in growing it. If we can grow it here or elsewhere, those residents of Pradang involved could become wealthy and the rest of our people would benefit from cheaper dilbar."

Siddathamon proved he was intelligent enough for the most prominent University in the galaxy by staring his *tailung* in the eye. "Is that the reason for the generous gift? You expect I'll find the secret to growing this dilbar, and make you even richer?"

Bardavong chuckled. "I see you're a good choice for my quest. Of course you would be included in whatever profit we can gain. Just be careful, others would like that kind of profit also." Bardavong then had a roboserver bring in some refreshments, and the conversation turned to academic comparisons of the college Bardavong had attended on Pradang versus the University so many lightyears away.

Siddathamon learned just how interested others were before he could even return home. On leaving the home of his *tailung* he boarded his surface car (not yet being old enough to be allowed any flying), and started the twelve kilometer trip. He had barely gone four kilometers when his car ceased to obey him. Doors were locked, windows sealed, his complink refused to function, while the surface car headed off in a strange direction. After about ten kilometers it drove into a cavernous building. Stopped. Doors still sealed. Windows on either side lowered, but not enough to slip out. Four large men approaching, two clearly carrying weapons. Siddathamon regretted not having devoted more effort to self defense classes. He carried nothing convincingly usable as a weapon.

"You will accompany us."

65

"Why? Who are you?"

"You will accompany us."

"Don't be silly."

The two holding weapons each shoved one into an ear. The one on the left was more painful. "Alright, I'll accompany you." The door released and he got out and followed/was led by the four. The group entered a room. Siddathamon was forcefully seated. A bright light shone on him. The rest of the room was dark. "What did your uncle ask you to do?"

"Who?"

A slap across the face. "Your uncle Bardavong. Don't play cute. We have no inhibitions about what state we leave you in if you won't co-operate."

"How unfortunate. Bardavong's offer of money to co-operate was much nicer, and that got my cooperation a lot faster."

"Really? How much?"

Siddathamon told himself these goons had to be off-worlders if they called Bardavong his 'uncle'. Let's see if they will make a counter offer. He tripled the amount his tailung had given him, then added 50 percent more. He heard grunts.

"What were you expected to do for such a fortune?"

"*Uncle* Bardavong wanted to be told immediately if I ever discover fossils of an intelligent species."

"Either he's crazy or you're lying. At least five million planets have been checked without any signs of intelligence. Here's what lies get you." The slap was a lot harder than he had expected.

"Uncle Bardavong was much nicer about it, in addition to the money."

"I'm not one of your relatives, and I never play nice. What did he want?"

"He wanted to be informed if in going to various worlds to explore for fossils I —"

The full room was suddenly illuminated. Hulking, uniformed figures holding nasty looking weapons poured in through two doors. A couple came through a disguised window Pretty had been unaware of. An obviously amplified voice said, "Drop weapons and hold your hands high. Failure to follow orders will result in severe consequences."

The one who had slapped Pretty responded, "If you want the kid back in one piece, back out of here." For emphasis he added, "May *sawfangs* eat your flesh." Pretty had never heard of *sawfangs*, but figured whatever they were, this revealed his kidnappers' home planet. It was his last thought before a popping sound closed all perceptions.

Pretty heard Bardavong's voice say "Are you awake yet?"

Pretty groaned dramatically. In part he even felt a groan was physically needed, other than seeking sympathy. Eyes squinted open. Back in Bardavong's home!

Bardavong said, "Don't worry. Effects of the gas used will wear off soon enough."

Pretty carefully sat up. "Who were those goons?"

"They'll be questioned separately when they awaken. Unlike you, we're not giving them any antidote to the gas, so that will be sometime tomorrow, and far more uncomfortable. The ones who are smart enough to answer our questions will have a somewhat longer and slightly happier life than the dumb ones."

"How did you manage to send in rescuers so fast? Was I followed, or did you set me up?"

"My dear *lungee* Siddathamon, when you are older and more mature, you'll know the answer to that."

"I'm already smart enough to figure out that they're from off-world."

"How do you know that?"

"They referred to you as my uncle!"

"What did they ask about *me*?"

"They wanted to know what you asked me to find, and how much money you offered. I more than tripled the amount, and told them you wanted to be the first told if I found fossils of an intelligent species."

"Intelligent..." Bardavong choked laughing uproariously, and could not finish speaking.

"Well, they called me a liar and started slapping me around. Your people broke it up before anything else happened."

"Did they tell you where they were from?"

"No, but I'm sure the reference to some sort of native nasty called a *saw fang* should provide all the clue you need."

"*Sawfangs,* eh? No, it doesn't tell us. They are a particularly large, efficiently clever, strong, and vicious animal that have made their planet basically unusable to humans. Don't worry about it, " he scowled, and added, "when we're done questioning they may wish they lived on the *sawfangs'* home world."

"Dilbar is really that valuable?"

"Unfortunately it is. Its by products provide the only known medicines for a number of neurological diseases. Anyhow, let's make sure you get home safely, and perhaps not tell your parents about this episode so they don't worry needlessly."

Pretty thought for a moment. Father was perfectly capable of cancelling his University plans if he thought going off world was dangerous. He nodded slowly to indicate agreement with his *tailung.* He considered for a moment suggesting this episode entitled him to a larger stipend from Bardavong, but decided this was not a favorable moment. Besides, he might sound greedy considering how large the original amount was.

Pretty was flown home by one of Bardavong's servants, while another took Pretty's ground transport back. His family accepted his story of thanking his *tailung* and then enjoying refreshments and a long conversation about off-planet education. Fortunately whatever medical treatment he received while unconscious had concealed the effects of the slaps.

Two days later Pretty embarked for the University, not nearly as sorry to leave Pradang as he had expected. His last look before boarding the spacecraft swept over his family, and took in the large planet Khodang in the sky.

This is an earlier adventure in the life of Pretty, who appeared
in the story "Beyond Space"in my earlier anthology *The
Mountain of Long Eyes.* Some think this next story about
Pretty may be negative.

A QUESTION OF TASTE

"Pretty, you're going to have to do some genuine field work to
complete your doctorate."

"The work back on Pradang wasn't genuine enough?"

"It's your home world, which opens questions of objectivity
and your ability to find and study new sites. You should've realized that, it's certainly been covered often enough in class lec-
tures and elsewhere, especially the rules for advanced degrees.
Anyway, we've found the perfect place for you."

Pretty, who was accustomed to using that nickname because
few off worlders could handle Siddathamon Priddikachorn, had
expected a demand for more field work, but had hoped to be
the one doing the choosing. "Where is this?"

"The Federation has been leaning on an unaffiliated world
called Giltine about 290 lightyears from here. It has an odd history. The original settlement came shortly after Mulvey's travel
methods were revealed, but they came as dissidents from a
fairly backward part of Earth, and no one knew or cared where
they had settled. About a century later some criminal group
found them and took over the planet. They stayed more or less
out of contact for quite a while after that, but around eighty
years ago began regular trade with Federation worlds, buying
mostly advanced tech consumer items, while selling luxury
food products based on some native species. They also export
some deuterium to worlds where it's in short supply naturally."

"I hope some of that assures fossils, so at least I won't be
wasting my time there." Prior to a dig on his home world of

Pradang Pretty had been to a planet where conditions seemed to have prevented the formation of fossils. This despite native life forms that appeared to have been around long enough for significant evolution to have taken place.

"Queen Cynthia's government was very reluctant to allow anyone in beyond the existing small diplomatic mission, but the Federation threatened trade sanctions, so they agreed to allow one xenopaleontologist fitting your description. They also will tell you exactly where you can search. You're allowed three months to seek fossils."

"Queen Cynthia, eh? Is she good looking?"

"We don't know what she looks like. Every off worlder who's ever seen her or any of her predecessors in the Bloor dynasty is dead. And they have a tradition of never showing photos of the ruler. Goes back a couple centuries to an era when assassination was more common."

"*Umm*! Maybe some nice lonely princesses eager to meet an off world scientist..."

"You'll have as little to do as possible with any of the human population on Giltine. Part of the problem is that descendants of the original colonists are reportedly still pretty much an underclass. The secret police are called 'The Vampires', and are bolstered by genetically enhanced dogs. Someone from the ruling group will direct you to your research sites, and they may well have a guard from the Vampires to keep you from straying."

"Oh, joy, a bunch of suspicious crooks with no knowledge of geology saying where to find fossils. Why am I cursed with this particular enterprise?"

"You were available and fit the profile of what Giltine said they would allow. And from your point of view it's an interesting introduction to the problems of field work."

"I take it 'interesting' is a synonym for gruesome."

Pretty's personal preparations needed only a brief time beyond the need to arrange the loan from his department of some specialized equipment. But being interviewed and investigated by Giltine authorities took weeks. Finally he boarded a Giltine vessel returning to the planet with a load of various consumer items. He was not surprised to learn he was the only passenger, and that the crew resented the cargo space his paleontological gear occupied. It was not a happy introduction to Giltine and its citizens.

On landing he was first met by a Giltine official. "You are Sitheemom Vreddykeechurn?"

Pretty figured, given the fate of those meeting the Queen, that correcting this stooge may not be worth the effort. "Yes."

The official waved a wand at Pretty. After a few moments the wand flashed green.

"How is it you have my biometrics?"

"You will open all cases and packages for inspection."

He sighed. They probably recorded him when he applied for this visit, back at the University. Now he had another worry. Some of the more delicate equipment would have to be repacked, and he wondered what the inspector understood of the equipment, or if he appreciated some of its fragility.

"Please to explain this device."

"I'm here to look for fossils. Many have a density different than that of surrounding rock. This device measures densities to a depth up to fifty meters, looking for hints of fossils from density fluctuations."

The next item was the inflatable housing Pretty would be using in the field. The stooge demanded it be inflated. Pretty could not resist saying, "It's larger on the inside than on the outside." The stooge looked confused, and carefully scrutinized every square centimeter of the outside, went inside for a prolonged inspection, and finally allowed it to be repacked.

"This device does what?"

"Here we have a oscillating magnetometer which functions to validate if previously detected fossils will have a composition commensurate with obligatory determinations of functionality." As hoped, the inspector's eyes glazed over, and he moved to something else.

After questioning a few more of Pretty's geological and paleontological gadgets, and getting responses which were progressively more vague and/or complex using possibly meaningless technobabble, the stooge finally ended his search. Pretty was next met by a member of the Federation's diplomatic staff. None of the staff came from Pradang, but with over 3500 inhabited worlds in the Federation, and only ten members in the diplomatic mission, that would have been against the odds.

"I assume you are Mr. Prittukaychern, here to conduct some geological studies. You are to accompany me to the embassy, where you will be briefed and given maps showing the areas the Giltine government has approved for your work."

"The name is pronounced Priddikachorn, and the studies are xenopaleontology, not geology. I trust the maps were not drawn up based on a fallacious assumption about geology, because if so I'm wasting my time here."

"You'll have to discuss that with the science attaché."

The two exchanged no further conversation for most of their way to the embassy. Pretty did his best to try to observe the architecture and the people they passed. The architecture had few unique features that he as a nonspecialist could recognize, and seemed built to withstand either ferocious weather or attacks. Finally he broke the silence to say, "I read that all dangerous native species are nearly extinct. Is that true?"

"A few are preserved in the Queen's private zoo. In the wild they are probably all extinct except for some ocean dwellers. Some nonthreatening native species are quasi domesticated and used for the export of exotic gourmet foods. You will have an opportunity to taste some at the formal reception scheduled tomorrow." He fell silent. Pretty thought about it, and decided the mission was probably so isolated that the visit of any off worlder was grounds for a party.

The diplomatic mission's entire staff of ten people greeted him, and after introductions he was shown to a temporary room. He would use this as housing until allowed to head for an area of possible interest. He relaxed on the bed, and wondered if the promised reception would be worth the time. Speculating was fruitless, so he turned to reading reports of recent digs on worlds around G8 stars similar to Giltine's, interspersed with memorizing some Giltine vocabulary. The grammar seemed very different from any language he had previously studied. About an hour later he was joined by the science attaché, and they had a brief conversation which confirmed he was to be directed to areas with good prospects for fossils.

The formal reception brought him face to face with a Giltine official introduced as Robb, Baron Gryll. The Baron said, "I understand you brought a device that can determine the density of rocks to a depth of fifty meters? Can it identify useful minerals? We may wish to purchase it from you."

"Such devices exist, but mine is not designed for that purpose, just for detecting possible fossils. Anyhow, I couldn't sell the one I have because it belongs to the University's paleontology department."

"Ah, so disappointing. And why are you so interested in fossils? Especially ones on alien planets?"

"Baron, I'm glad you asked. I'm hoping to develop a theory of how similar classes of stars affect evolution on their inhabited planets. I've already got enough information to show evolutionary parallels as stars begin to evolve off the Main Sequence, and..."

The Baron waved his hand, and turned to a passing servant, snatching something off the tray she carried. She made an obeisance and said something before moving on through the gathering with her offerings. The Baron completely ignored her actions. Pretty noticed her skin tone and hair color were quite different than the Baron's. An indicator of the two different ethnic groups settled here? "Here, try one of our excellent native foods, prepared with some delicious spices and a small infusion of wine." The Baron waved her back.

Pretty stared at the sample she offered. It seemed to be an ellipsoidal meat patty with a brownish crust resting on a rectangular wafer. On Pradang, except for fruits, nearly all foods were prepared and eaten in shredded form or in soups. Slowly he took the sample.

The young woman carrying the serving platter curtseyed deeply and said something in the Giltine language. Pretty turned to the Baron. "What was that?"

"She just thanked you for honoring her and her father by taking that food."

"Hah! We'll see how much honor is deserved by taking a bite." He had learned to accept a wide variety of foods from many worlds at the University, so screwing up his courage, Pretty took a bite. "Wow!"

"So, you like our native foods?"

"Like? It's delicious. I detect a hint of ginger, perhaps garlic, and what I assume are some native spices. I'm tempted to drop paleontology and go into business importing this to Pradang."

Baron Gryll laughed. "This is exported in small quantities, and I understand is quite expensive on Federation worlds."

"What about the meat? Could we export the animal this is made from?"

"The Hesat do not travel well, and would not reproduce in the Federation. But you should know that this is just one of our many excellent foods. This one tastes even better with a mustard sauce."

"Word of this gets out, you may have an influx of immigrants and tourists."

"Alas, Giltine is not open to either. Our population is delicately balanced on our resources, and the Queen's government does not welcome large numbers of off-worlders."

"May I ask about your government? I'm from Pradang, where we have an elected parliament that to be honest few bother to vote for or pay much attention to. Giltine seems to have preserved a really old fashioned type of government, with a queen and baron. Have you other inherited titles?" Another servant passed by, and Pretty seized a second helping. The servant bowed and said something that Pretty ignored as convincingly as any native Giltine aristocrat. Baron Gryll responded while Pretty seemed to eat the sample, but secretly pocketed a small portion.

"There are several different inherited titles of various ranks. It's one reason we never joined the Federation, which frowns on such things. Also, we have our own language and would be reluctant to switch to galstandard. May I ask about Pradang?"

"We've been settled for over 400 years, since shortly after release of how to do second level travel, and voluntarily joined the Federation when it was formed. Pradang has about 480 million people, even though it's not a planet."

"Not a planet? What is it? Surely you don't have the secret for living on a brown dwarf! I can't imagine a space station that large."

Pretty allowed himself to chuckle. "It's one of our jokes. Pradang orbits a super Jovian at a distance of about 13 million kilometers, and the Jovian is about 165 million kilometers from a G1 star, so technically we live on a moon, even though Pradang's diameter is actually a few hundred kilometers more than Earth's."

"Ah, and has this had any influence on your culture?"

"It might have inspired my interest in seeing how different types of planets and home stars influence the evolution of native life forms, which is why I'm on Giltine eating your delicious native foods instead of doing the research I was sent here to do."

The Baron smiled, and assured Pretty that he would be able to begin work within days. He did not, however, add, as Pretty discovered when he was finally guided to his first location, that the Baron would be with him the entire time. The Baron explained, as they flew to the site, that this region, called Ghoc, was a remote and hitherto worthless part of his estates.

At the first selected site Pretty looked around after the rather primitive helicopter dropped him off along with Baron Gryll, his scientific equipment, various supplies and one of the genetically modified dogs. The Baron said, "If you choose this place, it has always seemed pretty ordinary to my family. Certainly no bones lying around."

"Forgive me if I offend, but that's the sort of misunderstanding common among outsiders on how paleontology is practiced. Just let me set some of my machinery to work."

Pretty studied the reports his devices produced. "Okay, the local rocks seem to be sedimentary. That's a reasonable start, but far from an assurance of usable material." Gryll just watched. "We might have something at a depth of nineteen meters. Any problem if I send a probe down?"

Gryll shrugged. "It's what you came here to do. Her majesty's government knew that when your presence was approved. This is not a region with any known significant value. It's my property, and I certainly don't mind."

Pretty set up some equipment, worked a keyboard briefly, and stood back, watching a display screen. A thin flexible tube descended into the ground. After a couple minutes he shook his head. "Just a lump of granitic xenolith. Probably washed into the sediment by a flood."

"Your devices tell you this so quickly without you needing to look at a sample?"

"Some elements of my work are pretty routine."

The rest of the day proceeded in a similar manner, with nothing showing up that could reasonably be considered a fossil. Pretty did spot a collection of recent animal remains resembling seashells lying near a bush, and tried to surreptitiously pocket a piece. The dog, which stood 1.6 meters at the shoulder, growled a distinctly understandable "No." He stared, and turned to Gryll. "The dog talks?!"

The dog responded "Yes."

The Baron added, "Part of the genetic modifications; along with size, strength, and larger brains, it has humanoid vocal cords. Works wonders for aiding in controlling crowds and questioning suspects. This one was selected for our little expedition because he speaks Galstandard as well as our native language."

Pretty decided he would be unlikely to grab samples with this dog around, and said, "Would there be any problem if I collected a couple samples of recently deceased plants or animals? If we do find fossils, the current life forms would be of value in doing a contrast and analysis of recent evolutionary trends."

The Baron looked very doubtful. "Let me think about this. If you really need recent samples, we might want to provide them, rather than picking up junk here in the wild. Some of our native life emit hazardous toxins."

Pretty nodded. When Baron Gryll was not watching and the dog was elsewhere he slipped the piece of shell into an analyzer. Giltine's native forms seemed to agree with most of the rest of the galaxy that shells were best made with a calcium compound. He frowned at some of the other chemicals noted.

"Damn, I had forgotten. Your planet exports deuterium, so it must have a high percentage. My instruments were all set back at the University, where deuterium is one part in 8422 of hydrogen, so I'm getting some weird readings. The correct fraction is needed to determine ages on any samples I find. Would you know what fraction deuterium is here?"

The Baron looked blank. "I'll have to check for you." He pulled out a phone and dialed. He carried on a conversation in the Giltine language, apparently getting more and more annoyed. He finally shouted something into the phone in which Pretty thought he heard the name Cynthia included. Moments later he shoved the phone back in his pocket with a determined smile. "One part in 3019."

Pretty thanked him, and went to work revising the settings. He muttered to himself. The Baron said, "Excuse me? I did not understand."

"Nothing, just frustrated. It's not enough I have to know all sorts of things about hundreds of planets, I also get stuck with chemistry I am seriously not interested in. Ever hear of 'enol'?"

"I'm happy to say that being a Baron exempts me. So it's a chemical your instruments are having problems with?"

"I'm not sure. Just more work for the overburdened graduate student seeking to earn an honest PhD." Gryll looked puzzled for a moment and then decided the remark was meant as humor and smiled.

Pretty punched up his computer, and read that enol was a rarely found isomer of guanine, and that life forms from Earth and other planets with DNA or an analog used a more common guanine isomer called keto. He shrugged, and was about to move on when a stray though occurred to him. He pulled out the hidden food sample from the Embassy's welcoming party.

The computer confirmed the food sample's DNA analog used the keto isomer of guanine. He blinked in surprise, and then hid a sly grin. Finding a planet that used two different isomers would make him famous. The Baron noticed the grin. "A good result?"

"I hope so. The foods served back at the reception for me, were they all native to Giltine?"

"Yes, why? We do that for formal events as an honor to the guest." Baron Gryll appeared to be tensing.

"Are all your foods native or do you have things that originated on Earth or elsewhere?"

"Earth foods tend only to be eaten by the lower classes in most cases, except for wines and their brandy derivatives, and a few vegetables."

"With luck I might even detect what makes your local items so delicious."

The Baron seemed to relax a bit, but frowned. "I think you would be better advised to stick to seeking the fossils you came here for, and not concern yourself with our dietary practices." The dog added a growl.

That remark made Pretty curious, but he felt that not pursuing the issue with the Baron would be more productive, or at least safer. He shrugged, hoping it would be interpreted as marking a lack of serious interest.

That night he waited until the Baron and dog were undoubtedly asleep, and set up an analyzer. This he fed samples of various plants found in the area, tiny bits of the couple fossils so far retrieved, and samples of the food brought with them. Some of the food was native, the rest items Pretty had brought to Giltine. He stared at the results, somewhat perplexed. All the native plants and fossils without exception had the enol isomer of guanine, while the food, regardless of source, was the keto isomer. It finally dawned on him that probably humans could not properly digest the enol isomer, so it was no surprise all the food was keto. But why were none of the wild samples he had collected keto? Surely there should be some in the samples collected if native foods had it? He fell asleep pondering the issue.

The next two months were a somewhat routine sequence of setting up camp, running analyses for the presence of fossils, breaking down camp, and moving to a new site. The Baron soon picked up on what sorts of geography Pretty favored, and stops gradually became more productive of fossils ranging from a few million to several hundred million years in age. But none used the keto isomer.

His three months on Giltine were nearly ended. Baron Gryll pointed this out, and asked "Have you been able to collect enough fossils to help your studies? It means nothing to me, but after seeing how earnest and hard working you are I rather hope all that effort pays off. You nearly equal the diligence of some of our lower class, although I trust your work will be more productive."

"The biggest problem is straightening out some DNA isomers, but beyond the complications that introduces it looks to me like I've got what I need. Evolution of your native species should have some interesting results in a few tens of millions of years if my readings are correct."

"I doubt I'll be around to check on how accurate you are with that prediction. Will the University really confirm your degree on something so, mmm, speculative?"

Pretty smiled. "No need to be so polite. I know you think this is all nonsense, but xenopaleontology is becoming a fairly predictable science. Just a few things to clear up, and I can do all that using equipment I left back in the embassy. I'm sure you'll be delighted to go back to your normal life instead of having to tag along with me."

"It's not been so bad. I've had some easy lessons in geology, paleontology, all sorts of useless things I can use to impress people at parties."

"And I'll have credit for doing serious field work. Plus impress people with stories about your dogs and meeting a Baron. See, we both benefit from my having been here."

The dog growled without speaking. Both humans looked at him. Pretty, who was at last adjusting to its presence, said "And

I hope you enjoyed our travels also." The dog growled again without speaking.

The Baron addressed the dog, saying, "Is there some problem?"

"I cannot smell his fossils."

"Hardly surprising, they've been dead millions of years, and have mostly turned into stone."

"Some stones have smell."

"Mostly stones with smelly chemicals, or ones that have been lying near the surface and picked it up. Frankly, I'm glad fossils don't smell, since I'm going to have to share a cabin with the ones I've found on my way back to the University."

Gryll added "Your fossils will be inspected before you leave."

Pretty shrugged. "I found nothing of monetary value, if that's your concern. No gold, palladium, iridium, or uranium in my samples, just good honest fossils."

"It's not my choice. Planetary rules established long ago."

"I understand. No problem. I've heard of tougher rules on other planets, even a few on Federation members. If I were interested in stealing anything of value, I could have picked an easier method than learning xenopaleontology. Anyway, my family back on Pradang is quite well to do, and I have a wealthy uncle bankrolling a lot of my education."

"Lucky you. Being a Baron, my family had no money worries either."

"Would you like me to send you a courtesy copy of whatever I get published from my work here? Or even a copy of my thesis, assuming it's accepted?"

"I can't guarantee I'll read every word, or understand the parts I do read, but I would appreciate whatever you feel like sending. It will be a nice memento of our unusual adventures that I can use to prove I'm not lying when I brag about what we did together."

Pretty grinned, but did not comment, thinking about the contrast with the significance back at the University of his work. As he completed breaking down his final site a skinny, haggard looking man staggered from the forest. Seeing Pretty he called "Please...foreigner...we food...off world...help...food us". He got no further, as the dog leapt on him and in one swift act bit his head off. It then proceeded to start eating him.

Pretty turned away, sickened. Baron Gryll frowned. "It is illegal for Hesat to learn galstandard. Please don't get too upset. What do you think he wanted?"

"It sounded like he was begging for food, I think." Pretty reminded himself accidents could still happen, right up until he was back at the University. The Baron looked sharply at him, but seemed satisfied.

The inspection of his samples extended to looking at all of his equipment, and everything else he had brought with him and was taking back, including even his clothing. A couple items he had purchased to take back as gifts drew some raised eyebrows, but no objections. Finally Pretty was aboard a Giltine merchant vessel headed to the University planet.

His return to the University was largely ignored except for a demand for prompt return of the equipment he had borrowed. It took two days to get in to see his advisor. "Giltine is outrageous. Their main export has us eating part of their population. Why doesn't the Federation do something?"

"The Federation has never been able to prove anything to the point where everyone will believe it. And the independent worlds are more than prepared to act if the Federation leans too hard on one of their number."

"But this is disgusting."

"Now you begin to understand some of the problems of field work."

While some might think this is dated, given what is happening to our space program, I say you are very wrong. Besides, this is close to some real events

AMERICAN WINS 'HERO OF THE SOVIET UNION' AWARD

"Yes, kids, someday soon people will travel in space, and even land in places like the Moon. Did you know Jupiter has twelve moons? Imagine being able to explore all those."

"Gee, Phil, that sounds exciting." Paul's eyes were glowing.

"I dunno. What makes you so smart?" Rob was already starting to grow into being a neighborhood bully, and admiring someone not given to pumping iron or kicking smaller kids would spoil his image.

Phil smiled at Rob, and said, "I've got over a dozen books on astronomy at home, and I've read all of them, starting with *The Stars For Sam.* Of course, Jupiter and our moon aren't stars, but there are plenty of books about them."

Patsy said, "Have you ever seen Jupiter?" Rob frowned. He was far enough into puberty to resent an older kid impressing one of the girls.

"Loads of times with just my eyes, and a couple times with a brand new telescope my parents bought me. In fact, if it's clear tonight, you are all invited over to my house at 7:00 to use it to look at Jupiter and the Moon."

"An' what if it isn't clear?" Rob said with a distinct sneer. "You gonna claim clouds if your telescope don't work?"

"No, I have a Spitz Junior Planetarium, and we can use it to study what stars should be out tonight. Either way my mom's serving lemonade, chocolate milk, cookies, and her homemade pie."

The kids, except Rob, all cheered. The cheering was cut off when the teacher assigned lunchroom duty, Mrs. Prendergast, called them to line up to return to classes.

After all were in class Prendergast had to report to the Principal before taking her own lunch. "How was conduct during lunch today?"

"Excellent. Philip Dugan kept the other children quiet by telling them tales."

The Principal frowned in displeasure. "Dugan again? He's a seriously disturbed child who is dragging others into his fantasy world."

"Not this time. I heard nothing of fantasies, he was just giving the other children a science lesson."

"Science, or made up nonsense?"

"He told the children Jupiter has twelve moons. Even I didn't know that, I thought it just had four."

"See, fantasy! Do you believe everything a seventh grader says? So Jupiter has twelve moons? How would he know? Maybe if Dugan told the others that juries have twelve members, or there are twelve months in the year we could allow it, but even if Jupiter did have that many moons, what difference would it make? We can't have Dugan filling the other children's heads with nonsense, especially nonsense about irrelevant things. We have a responsibility to parents and the School Board to educate properly."

"Would you rather I prevent these little lunch time seminars of his?"

"Definitely. And if he tries this at other times, let me know so we can put a stop to it."

The night was clear, but by 8:10 o'clock the Dugan adults felt the children should come inside, luring them with the promised goodies. Their son used the time to show off his small planetarium, which his father had enhanced with a small reddish light to simulate twilight. Well before 9 the children were sent on their way home, thrilled with the things they had seen and heard about even though keeping the telescope aimed, and refocusing for each kid, ate up much of the time.

The children except for Rob. He had given himself a stomach ache from gorging on the goodies the children had shared. And he hated that Philip was gaining popularity. His chance came thanks to his bullying. Two days after the sky party Rob amused himself at school by taunting a second grader, who ran back to her classroom crying. When her teacher heard that Rob was the one who had made her cry the Principal was notified. Rob was soon in the Principal's office.

"Rob, what's this I hear about you teasing a second grader? You're a big boy, and shouldn't pick on children so much smaller than you."

"Ah, I wuzn't teasin' her. I was tryin' a tell the kid about what Dugan did a couple nights ago, an' it seemed to scare her."

"Philip Dugan? What did he do?" The Principal seemed to have forgotten Rob's alleged infraction, so eager was he to hear about Philip Dugan.

"He had a bunch o' kids at his house for cookies and stuff. Sumpin' was wrong with it 'cause I got a stomach ache. Anyhow, he turned out the lights and had this thing he called a planetarium to show the sky, even though outside it was clear."

"Alright, Rob. In the future don't tell younger children things that may upset them. Now go back to class, and study hard."

Rob left the office smirking to himself. The Principal prepared a letter to send to the Dugan parents, asking them to come to his office for a conference. The meeting took place a couple days later.

"Your son is not only disrupting classes with his fantasies, but I am informed some of those fantasies are frightening younger children. This must stop immediately or I will be forced to suspend him from school indefinitely."

Philip's mother immediately said, "We'll definitely tell him not to discuss anything other than school work."

"That's a good start, but you must go further and discourage his fantasies, or we will have to recommend him for psychological counseling, and having that in his record could well make it impossible to gain admission to a good college, should that be your future plans for him."

Philip's father leaned forward. "How would you have us discourage him? I'm not in favor of physical punishment for this. What makes you so certain this is a problem?"

"No, I don't think physical punishment would be appropriate, and quite possibly would not be effective. I learned the dangers of living a fantasy life from an uncle. He nearly memorized all the Oz books from reading them so often, and dragged some of my older cousins to see the movie a dozen times. He was waiting to be deployed to England during the war when he choked to death on his own vomit in a Chicago drunk tank. So you can see where living outside the bounds of the real world can lead. You must bring all the books or other printed materials Philip uses for his fantasies, plus his telescope, and what I hear is a small planetarium, to the school. We will have you destroy all of this in front of a school assembly to let all the children know that this is unacceptable."

Both parents vigorously objected, Mr. Dugan commenting that the books, telescope and planetarium had together cost close to a hundred dollars. Mrs. Dugan said it was just a way for Philip to play.

"This is a very dangerous form of play because it is psychologically unhealthy. And I fear that you have both been co-operating in encouraging his unrealistic behavior. By destroying the implements personally at a school assembly you will be showing Philip and all the other children that adults cannot tolerate the way he has been misleading the other children. After these things are destroyed, you should get him some books that are acceptable reading, such as Booth Tarkington, and safe toys like cap pistols. I have to warn you, if this does not work, I cannot allow Philip in the building. Instead I will have to send him to our school district's program for disturbed and dangerous children. Perhaps we can still save him from my uncle's fate if you cooperate."

The following Monday a school wide assembly gathered to watch as the Principal introduced the Dugans as Philip's parents. A school aide brought out a basket holding several books, went off stage, and brought back a rectangular blue box with the words "Spitz Junior Planetarium" on it. The third trip brought out a small telescope and tripod.

The Principal went to the podium again. "Philip Dugan has been disrupting classes and school discipline with fantasies and disruptive behavior involving the materials you can see on this stage. His parents have agreed with me that in order to preserve discipline, return Philip to reality, and guide all the children in this school towards a better education, all these things should be destroyed. The books will be taken outside, and burned." He paused and nodded to the aide, who picked up the basket of books and walked out of the auditorium. "Mr. and Mrs. Dugan will now destroy the other offending items. I should add that were this not done, Philip would be unable to remain in this school as a student." Sitting far to the side of the auditorium Philip quietly cried.

The school year ended five weeks later. Philip never once in those five weeks said a single word in the school, and was noticeably silent at home and elsewhere.

The new school year began early in September. Rob tried to heckle Philip a few times, but finding he never responded in any way eventually sought more rewarding prey. On the evening of October 4 broadcast media carried news of the launch of a "Russian rocket put a thing they were calling a Sputnik into space." The next day at school, a Friday, the principal briefly used the school's classroom address system to tell students that if they had heard of this, it was most likely a lie because claims to travel in space were nonsense they should ignore, and stick to approved school work. Philip listened to this without showing a visible reaction.

The local town newspaper's staff had a couple children in the school, so they heard about the principal's remarks, and a small blurb appeared in the paper with an approving editorial.

On October 17 the school secretary was sorting the day's mail. She called the Principal's attention to an unusual envelope. "This letter is addressed to you. It has a return address of the Soviet consulate in Manhattan."

"Now isn't that odd. Let's see what this is all about." He opened the envelope and scanned the letter inside. "I seem to be invited to a ceremony to be held at their Manhattan consulate to receive an award as a Hero of the Soviet Union for my contributions to their science program. What in the world is that all about?"

"When is the award ceremony? And does the letter say what the award consists of?"

"The ceremony is at my convenience, although they suggest during our Christmas/New Year's break. No indication what the award consists of beyond the title."

"Do you want me to send a letter proposing a date?"

"Not at all. I don't need the controversy of accepting an award from the Soviet Union. Type up a letter expressing my profound appreciation of the honor, blah, blah, blah, but the rules of our local school board do not permit personnel to accept outside awards."

"Oh, my, I didn't know that!"

"That's because there is no such rule. but it sounds like a perfect excuse to avoid publicity that might make people call mea pinko. I don't know what I might've done to make them think I've helped their quote science program unquote, but it's all nonsense anyway. No one's ever going into space, and this so-called Sputnik is probably a hoax. I just hope that Philip Dugan doesn't use this foolishness to start making trouble again."

This owes itself to Fredric Brown, who wrote the first two sentences as the shortest SF story ever told. *Twilight Zone* **and others have provided explanations for what happens after the knock. Here's mine.**

THE LAST MAN

The last man on Earth sat in his room. There was a knock on the door.

"It's not locked, it's never locked."

The door opened. The last woman on Earth stood there. "I know I said I wouldn't have you if you were the last man on Earth. "I've changed my mind."

TOURISM

"Welcome to Galactic Reality Adventures. We are delighted to host so many of you who reject the pseudo adventures offered by Stellar Virtual Trips. Today we will be landing on a planet discovered 18 *hranqs* ago, and declared open for visits six *hranqs* ago.

"No, I'm sorry, I have no idea how *hranqs* may translate into your planet's time measurements. *Hranqs* are a standard galactic unit.

"As I was saying, this planet has been open for a fairly short time. Many of its native life forms are still active and not expected to be extinct for at least another three or four *hranqs*. While they are still active you can have the thrill of the hunt, and if the proteins are compatible, you can even learn the taste of your selected prey.

"This planet has extensive sections covered with water—that's dihydrogen oxide for those of you from planets lacking the molecule. Those from planets with water may enjoy entering it and hunting some of the remaining life forms there, although I'm told all the larger ones are already extinct.

"The atmosphere is compatible for everyone approved for this tour. It would certainly depress our sales staff if it got out that we allowed our patrons to choke on incompatible air.

"The portal is through the gate behind me. You will be met on the other side by your tour guide and by a certified huntsman who will aid you in tracking the very best in astonishing alien creatures. Please do not get upset if you find any of the creatures on the planet you are about to visit revolting, disgusting or of a nauseating appearance. Remember, every creature is beautiful to itself, and if that doesn't work for you, well, you will soon be leaving these things behind, and will have marvelous memories and images to show off at home. Imagine how you will brag about facing down some of the most loathsome looking creepy crawlies anyone from your species has ever seen. And maybe even eaten one.

"So please line up for transferring through the portal."

***

"Alright, those of you with legs, please move to the right. Those who slither can follow them. Anyone find the gravity here too strong?"

"Fine, we have mobility devices for you. Please adjust to your own comfort, and remember not to let your grav field interact with any one else's."

"No madam, you will not be harassed by the galactic preservationists if you collect some trophies. The Council has ruled this planet's lifeforms are too offensive to preserve."

"That rubble you see in the distance used to be one of the main cities of the planet. Unfortunately the radioactivity levels will remain lethal for at least eight more hranqs."

"An interesting question, sir. Yes, this planet has a satellite, and for a small additional charge we will be delighted to take you there and show you some primitive artifacts left by the locals."

"We hope you will all enjoy your visit, and tell your friends this planet remains available to all visitors who can tolerate the atmosphere and temperature range."

I actually started this story on a manual typewriter during the last apparition of Halley's Comet in 1986. This is shorter and cleaned up. Hope you think it is worth the revamp.

THE VISITOR

Slowly, slowly I became aware. What caused awareness? I have never learned. From the slowness? Other reasons? At that distant time my thoughts were slow, but even today I am slow except when nearest the Heat. For many long ages I remained far from the Heat, circling it. At that time I did not think of it as the Heat, for heat was unknown to me. I did, however, gradually become aware of others similar to myself circling the Heat at a great distance. These others rarely came close enough for me to learn much about them. At that time it never occurred to me that we might communicate. Yet I found they were in some ways made of materials similar to myself. Most were considerably smaller than me, and I came to develop a theory that two (or more?) of these bodies may have collided, and so created me. Against this theory I admit to having twice observed two collide, and each time instead of forming a single larger body, they shattered.

I have much time to think, so even though I think slowly, I am able to think greatly. I learn there are more than ninety kinds of small particles—today I call them atoms. The most common type of atom within me is the lightest of all, so I call it number one. Number one combines with many of the others, often in very complex compounds, other times in very simple ones.

Thus time passed. After awareness came I circled the Heat over four hundred times. Studying myself kept me interested for much of that time, and if it became dull there was much else to think about. Finally, though, there came the event which changed my life forever. An object nearly as large as I, and apparently possessing greater mass, passed so close to me that we could not have placed anything my size between us.

The other pulled on me with the same force that the Heat had used for so long to make me circle it. But I did not circle the other. Instead my path about the Heat was changed. I still moved about the Heat, but not a circle, instead in a great ellipse.

This ellipse allowed me to meet the giant ones who circle near the Heat. And all the giant ones except the two nearest the Heat have their own smaller companions circling them as they circle the Heat. I wonder why two lack companions. Their closest neighbor has but one. Perhaps being near the Heat discourages such companions.

I notice the largest giants also have rings about them. But I spend little time near any of the giants. I feel the giants pull on me with the same force as the Heat. Do they wish me for a companion? But they are too weak. The Heat is strong and continues to hold me.

But horror! As I move nearer the Heat I feel some of my material leaving me. It is mostly material of the number one atom combined with a single other atom, either numbers six, seven or eight. There is also a minor loss of other compounds. I am shrinking as a stream of lost material pours out from me, trailing away from the Heat as though once freed, now fears the Heat! I have learned not a fact, but an emotion: fear. Will I lose awareness as I shrink? I pass the Heat at about the same distance as the sixth giant, and head back to the cooling distance, still aware, but fearing a return to the Heat.

I leave the giants far behind as I return to the region where I had for so long circled the Heat. I arrive close to the point where I had met the other who had so disasterously changed my path. In those days I had thought of myself as circling the brightest light, but that no longer seems adequate. I name it the Heat, and worry about what will happen if I return near the Heat. I lost little material this time, but what of the future?

As I re-enter the familiar cold regions I notice a new worrisome effect. I am moving much slower than when I was here previously. Thus I realize I am permanently in a new path about the Heat. Gradually I use this to learn something of the force by which the Heat controls all its companions. The force weakens by the square of one's distance from the Heat. But there is no escaping the force.

I continue to go around the Heat in this new path. Each time I approach the Heat I lose a small amount of material. Each time I observe the giants and their companions from a great distance. On my eleventh time my path is changed again, this time when the largest giant uses the same force as the Heat. But it fails to make me its companion, as I see another giant has done to one of my fellows. Instead I am in a path which brings me even closer to the Heat. Now I approach it as closely as the eighth giant, and only get as far as the second giant. The second giant's path takes it once around the Heat while I make more than two of my new paths round it. The eighth giant circles the Heat more than 120 times for one of my paths.

My shorter path gives me more opportunities to examine the giants even as my nearness to the Heat makes my awareness speed up. The eighth giant is of little interest because it is always hidden beneath clouds. The companion of the seventh giant, like the companions of most of the giants, seems dull because it never changes. But its giant is fascinating. Much of its surface appears to be covered with one of the forms of the combination of the first and eighth atoms. Some even floats above the surface in the form it takes when it escapes from me near the Heat. Except near the poles, or floating above the surface, the compound is in a form I am unfamiliar with, neither ice nor vapor. I name this anomalous ice.

The sixth giant is covered with compounds of the eighth and twenty sixth atoms, which give it an odd color. At the poles I find ice. The companions are both small, dark, and do not interest me.

The fifth giant is the largest. It has many companions, both large and small. Only one, nearest to the giant of its four large companions, is interesting. Every time I pass near enough to observe, this companion has clouds rising above it, and a surface which constantly changes. This and the next companion are the only companions I can observe that lack craters. I have seen many collisions that cause new craters. I wonder how these companions avoided them. Their giant is cloud covered and I study the changing clouds with a new emotion. I name it awe.

The fourth giant has the most rings, mostly tiny pieces of ice. There is no anomalous ice here. I do not like looking at this giant's rings, as they make me think of the ice I lose when I am near the Heat.

The other three giants and their companions are not very interesting, and the rings of the second and third upset me.

Gradually I concentrate my interest on just two giants, the largest and the seventh. Each is always changing, and the largest has many of the compounds that I am made of. On the giant they seem usually to be in the form they take when I am losing them near the Heat. Yet this giant is so far from the Heat that I am barely disturbed, and the giant itself does not seem to be a small Heat. Why then do its compounds react this way? Could I somehow get material from the giant to replace what I have lost?

The seventh giant's surface is complicated. In addition to the normal ice and anomalous ice, parts of its surface are clearly not made of either kind of ice. These parts change color, now brown, then green, sometimes even showing ice. I name it the variable areas. On another pass I notice some of the variable areas have patterns of squares and rectangles. No other giant, and none of their companions, show these.

On my next few passes I see the amount of surface on the seventh giant with squares and rectangles has increased. I feel I must more carefully study this giant's surface. Another great surprise! There are many very tiny things on it which seem to have the ability to move independently. There are several large and many small variable areas on this giant, but the greatest part of its surface is covered with anomalous ice. The tiny independent mover are found in nearly all the variable areas, and even in some of the anomalous ice, but none I can find in the normal ice. This gives me much to think about.

In the eastern part of the largest variable area I discover the movers, as I name them, are watching me! I pass too far from the giant to study more.

It occurs to me to study the giants and their companions more carefully to learn if there are movers on their surfaces. I find no movers elsewhere, not even on the companion of the seventh giant. Of course, the surface of the eighth giant and the largest companion of the fourth are hidden by clouds, but movers seem to be a rare phenomenon.

As I move again to the cooling distances of the third and second giants I ponder the mystery of the movers. They seem to act, sometimes, in concert. This suggests that they are aware, as am I, and that they have a way of exchanging information with one another. Is there some way I could exchange information with them or with those similar to myself? I cannot think of any way to do that with either. I cannot even think of how the movers do that with one another, or how I could make them know I am aware. Perhaps on some future visit to their giant I will solve this.

On my next visit to the seventh giant I again attract much interest from the movers. Several travel from the eastern part of the largest variable area to a small area in the far west surrounded by anomalous ice. Here are stones piled into groups of three that are arranged in a circle. Many movers gather here to watch me. I feel great frustration (a new emotion I have just named) at my inability to think of a way to exchange information. I cannot understand how the movers seem to do that, but of course I also cannot understand how they move without the force from the Heat. I have found they seem to have no ability to move except along the surface of their giant. Perhaps the giant rules them in some manner different than how the Heat controls me.

Two visits later, when I am already approaching the path of the third giant, a new starflares briefly near the great band of stars which circles the sky. The thought occurs to me that if the movers like to study things in the sky, they might even now be looking at this temporary star. Too bad I am too far to know. The following visit the seventh giant's companion, hitherto a dull uninteresting place, has a bright new crater. This crater will be invisible to the movers, being on the side of the companion always facing away from its giant.

I wonder if I am becoming obsessive over the mystery of the movers. I have understood almost nothing about them, and they are occupying almost all my thinking now. However, thinking about them is better than worrying about what the Heat does to me.

On my next approaches I see movers using their tubes to travel west across one of the places of anomalous ice. Some of the tubes do something I cannot determine to other tubes. Many tubes seem to be destroyed. One mover is separated from the others, and waves to me! Can we at last communicate? Other movers have on many visits seemed to view me the way I regard the Heat. I am more confused than ever.

A new visit, and the movers surprise me again. I had realized many visits earlier that the movers, perhaps due to their small size, lacked the acuity of my perceptions. It appears they have also realized this, and have developed means to improve their limited perceptions. Movers from several places point what may be sticks at me. Another mover seems to have determined how the Heat controls me. That is very clever for a mover whose distance from the Heat hardly changes. Sometimes I think I should have concentrated on studying a simpler giant, or even one of their companions. But most of these are so simple to be of little interest. Actually, these puzzles excite me.

Since a mover had worked out my path on my last visit, I am not surprised to find my next visit is anticipated, and hundreds of movers are pointing their perception sticks at me. I do not disappoint them. The plume from the gasses I lose to the Heat is larger than usual.

Another visit and now thousands of movers point their perception sticks at me. I continue to try to find a way to communicate. I try to control the gasses leaving me, but fail. I note a few movers have found a way to rise above the surface. I depart from the seventh giant still thwarted, but a bit of my lost gasses brush across the giant. I wish I could tell the movers to return this to me, as I estimate in another sixty visits I will have lost a dangerous amount of material.

The next visit the movers have a new surprise. Five small objects leave the seventh giant and head for me. There are no movers with these objects, so presumably they again show they have solved the problem of communication. I detect very feeble energy flows from the objects back to the giant, and watch as some of the objects pass near me, while others pass through the plume of material I am losing. All five quickly leave me, just as I quickly pass their giant. I am intrigued to see that while the movers act independently of the Heat's pull, their objects are as ruled by it as I am.

Several movers are in two objects above their giant, also studying me. If they can leave their giant, why did they not accompany the objects which visited me? How did they negate their giant's force? I look forward to my next visit to this giant. Perhaps by then the movers will visit me directly and help solve the problem of communicating. Meanwhile I study how I might duplicate the feeble energies their objects made.

A new excitement when I next am near the second giant, as another object from the seventh giant flies past me. Again no movers, but feeble energies sent toward the giant. After leaving me, a brief plume and it escapes the Heat forever.

My next visit I find movers on their giant's companion. They and movers on the giant and in the space around it study me. I detect more of the feeble energies, which clearly are involved in their communications. I am working to learn how to join these communications.

As I again am pulled in toward the Heat I discover movers on one of the companions of the fifth giant. And even more on the sixth giant. Much of the feeble energies. As an experiment I make a bit of the energies, but receive no response. Many movers travelling between their giant and its companion, which has even more movers. So much of the feeble energies that I finally begin to understand their meanings!

Movers approach me. They place objects on me even as I expand my understanding of their communications. The objects left on me send out some messages, which I try to understand. As I approach the path of the eighth giant the movers all withdraw. This seems odd given their weaker perceptions. A strong energy field sent to the seventh giant, its companion, the sixth giant, and the companion of the fifth giant. At last enough strong data. I now understand their communications. "People of the Solar System, our most famous traffic hazard will now be destroyed."

"No, you must not d...."

Part Two: Non-Fiction?

APOLLO MEMORIES

The approach of the fiftieth anniversary of the first manned landing on the Moon has me thinking of my experiences then.

In 1962 I was working my first job out of college, writing manuals on programming for a major computer manufacturer, even though my degrees were in German and astronomy. I was not happy in this job, and let various people I knew socially about this. A lawyer I was acquainted with passed this along, and one day I received a phone call from an engineer, Jerry Cook. He said he worked at Grumman Aircraft, which had just received the contract to build the lunar lander. He asked if I would be interested in working on the Apollo Project.

My response was that I would trade an arm and both legs for the opportunity. He laughed, and acknowledged that I sounded interested. Being hired took two months. All my mother's neighbors were interviewed by the FBI (which titillated everyone in her apartment building). Then at Grumman I was asked to look at an incredibly long list of organizations and indicate if I or any relative is or had been a member, followed by a catch all question regarding membership by myself *or any member of my family* in any organization not listed that "advocated the violent overthrow of the government", with threats of civil and criminal penalties for lies or omissions.

Not one to endanger myself with a lie or omission I wrote that my great great great great grandfather had loaned his second best horse to a notorious radical, who used it to ride through the Massachusetts countryside warning subversives that government soldiers from the Boston garrison were on their way. Days later his father (my five greats) fired a musket at government troops marching from Boston to a hill where insurrectionists had barricaded themselves.

The Head of all security at Grumman called me in and said he could not submit this because it would cause problems. I insisted that the terms of the security form required me to provide this information since the events took place in April

101

of 1775, when the government was the British Empire. Then I asked if it would cause *him* a problem? He shrugged and said "No." The form went in as written, and I never heard another word.

So what were the secrets I needed a security clearance for? Some details of the Saturn V rocket, which was being built in California by a different company, and which I never got near. The radio frequencies to be used for communicating with the astronauts. This was so every ham operator on Earth would not clog the airwaves trying to speak with them. And the planned launch schedules so the Soviets could not beat us to the Moon by a month. Since all this is so far in the past I can legally say the original intended date for the first landing was May 1967. The Apollo fire pushed that way back.

Once working on Apollo I was in group of about 40, mostly engineers of one sort or another, plus a couple draftsmen, a mathematician, a couple secretaries, and a lone astronomer— me. One of the secretaries said her previous job had been as a Playboy bunny in Manhattan. I had eaten there frequently, and asked what name she had used. She had been Bunny Ditto. I didn't recognize her or the name.

I found the engineers had invented their own vocabulary for much of the work. In need of some help I finally asked what this "central angle" was that they talked about so much. As soon as it was explained I said, "Oh, you mean the true anomaly." These poor semi-educated engineers, not knowing astronomical usages common since Kepler, had valiantly tried to invent already long established nomenclature.

The engineers came to me with their complaints about astronomers, also. In the early 1960s the distance to the Moon was well known to vary due to the Moon's elliptical orbit, but the values were known only to an accuracy of about one mile. When the engineers complained my only reply was that if the astronauts were going 240, 000 miles, and one mile made a significant difference, their tolerances were much too tight.

But I had to determine the tolerances for the accuracy of the on board radar, mainly during the orbital rendezvous between the orbiting Command Module and the returning Lunar Module, as well as the fuel usage during these maneuvers. The radar was built by an RCA facility in Massachusetts, and I got friendly with their liaison at Grumman.

By the time the Apollo 11 landed I was working for a planetarium manufacturer, writing canned shows they provided and sold with their planetariums (two free with the planetarium, buy the other three dozen). On July 19 I declared a Landing Party. A friend brought his television, so with mine we always had two of the then three networks covered. If one went to a commercial or dared cover other news we switched to the third network. About two dozen of my friends were present as Armstrong made the first human footprint on the Sea of Tranquillity, and while I had fully expected all terrestrial communications to suddenly be seized by aliens announcing we had qualified for junior membership in a galactic federation, the excitement prevented any disappointment.

FRAUDS IN ASTRONOMY

There is a certain charm to many frauds and fakes. The con man concept is a lot older than the Nineteenth Century story of the Confidence Man, and plays well in American fiction, including movies and television. But it's not so funny for those who fall for a scam and lose money to it. Astronomy has been one of the fields where frauds have accumulated.

The 1835 Moon Hoax was perpetrated by Richard Adams Locke to build circulation of the newspaper he was editor of. I feel astrology constitutes a hoax, but that is a sufficient topic all for itself. And there are those who claim the Apollo moon landings were a hoax, a claim which is itself a hoax, but since there is little money to be made from it (except for selling non-sensical books to the gullible), I'll leave that for another time.

Especially near Christmas we hear radio advertising offering to sell the right to name a star. For a not too outrageous price (except that any money wasted on a scam is outrageous) a star will be given the name you select, and you will receive a certificate, a celestial map showing the location of your star, and perhaps a copy of a book listing your star, its co-ordinates, and the name you selected, along with the stars and names a bunch of other people picked. And, the advertising promises, all this will be placed on file with the U.S. government!

All that is true, but it leaves out a few points. One is that the star will be one you will never see, unless you have access to a large telescope. The stars named are all very faint, not visible to the unaided eye. The government agency the names are filed with is the Copyright Office, because the law requires that any copyrighted work must have two copies provided. This was originally done to build up the Library of Congress cheap. It also keeps the Library abreast of everything published in the USA. The law does not, however, require the Library of Congress to hold onto everything. Works regarded as worthless are tossed out, and these star name volumes are all tossed.

Billions of stars have been catalogued by astronomers. Nearly all get catalog numbers, such as HD 28318 (the 28, 318th star in the Henry Draper Catalog), SAO +38 2515 (the 2515th star at 38 degrees north of the celestial equator in the Smithsonian Astrophysical Observatory catalog), Wolf 359 (the 359th star in Wolf's catalog of red dwarf stars), or 61 Cygni (the 61st star in Flamsteed's catalog of stars in the constellation of Cygnus).

About 800 stars have been given real names. About half of these are oriental, and used by no one outside of China or Taiwan. Most of the remainder are derived from Arabic, and describe either the constellation (e.g. Dubhe = bear in Arabic, a star in Ursa Major), or the star's location in the constellation (e.g. Betelgeuse, from an Arabic phrase meaning armpit of the giant). A very few stars have been given a name such as Barnard's star. In virtually every such case, the name honors an astronomer who either discovered the star or studied it and found it had some unique feature.

All celestial names have to be approved by the International Astronomical Union, the world-wide professional body of astronomers. The IAU has special commissions which examine proposed names, which have to meet certain standards. Comets usually get named for their discoverers (Halley's Comet is an exception, as it was known for many centuries).Discoverers of asteroids nowadays have a few guidelines limiting their choices for names. There is no chance whatsoever that the IAU would ever approve naming millions of stars in ways that smack of commercialism. But, sadly, some deluded souls appear at planetariums or observatories with certificate in hand, and ask to be shown "their" star. The sad thing is that the largest category of purchased names are for deceased children by bereaved parents.

At least people who "buy" a homestead on Mercury do so realizing it is just a good-humored way of donating money to the planetarium running this program.

Then there are the hoaxes involving UFOs. I used to know a fellow who had excellent and convincing photos of a flying saucer (a hub cap tossed in the air) firing a beam (touched up negative) at his elementary school, which was bursting into flames (composite photo). It looked like curtains for sure for the school, but I had relatives living near the school, and in driving by, I never saw a scorch mark from the beam.

Roswell and Area 51 figure in a lot of mythology. But in the very unlikely case that the U.S. government really is holding an alien spacecraft and the bodies of dead aliens, we show few effects in our technology of having learned anything. I might say something similar about those who claim contact, or, better yet, abduction on a UFO. No one ever manages to grab a souvenir, take a photo, or otherwise have some proof beyond a message along the lines of "Klaatu Barata Nicto".

Several times in recent years, usually around August emails were sent to thousands of people warning them that Mars would be visible in the sky in October, bigger and brighter than the Moon. Since Mars is almost exactly twice the Moon's size (4260 miles vs. 2160 miles diameter), to appear larger than the Moon, Mars would have to be less than twice the Moon's distance. The Moon's greatest distance in its elliptical orbit is about 252, 000 miles, so Mars would have to be 500, 000 miles or less from Earth to appear larger than the Moon. The trouble with this is that Mars can never get less than 34 million miles from Earth. And a good thing too. Imagine what having Mars within half a million miles of Earth would do to our tides! I wonder how many disappointed people stared into the sky, and then sent back a nasty email to the person who tricked them.

Back in 1910 some wise guys sold "comet pills" and "comet elixir" to protect people from the frightful effects of Halley's Comet as it passed near the Earth. Fortunately both the pills and elixir were so effective that even those who didn't spend any money on them were saved.

For a while there was quite a stir over a "face" seen on Mars by the Viking orbiters. Photographs showed a slightly blurry human face covering an area about a mile across, not far from what looked like large pyramids. Books were written, and NASA was denounced for keeping secret the evidence this was made by aliens. Alas, later mapping satellites took new pictures with much better resolution, and showed the face was just a jumble of hills, gullies, and sand dunes. No pyramids, either.

If we stop to think logically, why would NASA conceal the discovery of alien artifacts? Certainly if mile-wide alien constructions were to be found on Mars, there would be less controversy and more effort devoted to sending a crew there to investigate.

But I am afraid many people never look at things logically, or most hoaxes would be ignored. (Why would Mars, which has never been more than a bright dot in the sky suddenly appear larger than the Moon? How does a private firm get the right to name stars when the firm has no involvement in the field of professional astronomy?) Who discovered comets were hazardous, and created the pills and potions to counter-act the effect? Was the Great Stone Face at Franconia Notch, New Hampshire (recently destroyed) a sign aliens were in New Hampshire leaving proofs of their visit?

THE BIRTH OF THE SPACE AGE

On October 4, 1957 the Soviet Union launched the world's first artificial satellite, Sputnik 1. At just under two feet in diameter and weighing 184 pounds, it was a minimal effort by today's standards, as it circled the Earth broadcasting a plaintive "beep—beep".

Columbia University's ham radio station, W2AEE, taped the signal from Sputnik 1 as it rose above the horizon of New York City for the first time. This tape then went one block to Colmbia's FM radio station, WKCR, which became the first radio station in the United States to rebroadcast the Sputnik signal. The next morning, just after 9 am, the FBI stole the tape. Two of their agents simply walked into the station and demanded it. No payment, no return, no substitute tape.

I was a Columbia sophomore taking astronomy and working in the News Department of WKCR at this time. (This event influenced my subsequent career, as I worked on the Apollo Project and was an invited observer for the first fly-by of both Mercury and Saturn. I also spent 34 years teaching college astronomy.) The next meeting of astronomy classes saw Professor Jan Schilt walk into the lecture hall, and with a big grin he said "Well, gentlemen, it is not every day we have something new in the sky to discuss." He then spent the entire class period showing how the Soviets had deliberately launched Sputnik 1 into an orbit where it would not be visible in the night sky for the United States for about six weeks.

But the FBI should finally return that tape. The Soviet Union no longer exists and countries as small as Israel and North Korea launch satellites these days, so it is hard to imagine the tape contains any super secret national security information.

FRIENDS, OUR SKIES HAVE SOME PROBLEMS!

With the opening of the Creation Museum in Kentucky that incorporates a planetarium promoting creationist concepts of the universe, we are likely to see even more misunderstandings and warped views not just of science, but specifically of astronomical topics. The situation was already bad enough, if questions posted by some of the many thousands who use Yahoo's answer service are typical of the general public's knowledge and opinions regarding astronomical topics. Some questions there prove a little knowledge is very dangerous to one's understanding.

Consider the following question, which was really posted recently: "Could the Sun grow from hydrogen released by other planets like the Earth?" Given that the Sun is more than a thousand times the mass of the planets, this seems hardly significant. But the question was followed by this: "The Sun's mass unless I'm not aware of something new about physics is not a measurement. It's rather an answer written from newtonian math, and scientists doubt that Newton is totally right. Consider too that heated hydrogen inflates, hence a volume advantage to the Sun." I hardly know where to begin in critiquing this, so I'll just mention that astronomers routinely cite stellar masses in units of the Sun's mass.

Certain questions are constantly repeated: "why is the sky blue", "is Pluto a planet?" These are not too bad. I've even seen people coming up with Olbers' paradox on their own as a question. I would rate anyone who can do that as highly intelligent, if a bit under-informed. But what to make of those who cite the Mayan calendar and ask if the world will really end in December 2012? Do we really have worshippers of Kukulcan and Chaac going on line to seek reassurance about the longevity of the current cycle of the universe? Other worriers ask "Will the Moon ever explode and crash into the Earth?"

For a total lack of understanding, I would rate this highly: "Can the Sun be put out by water?" More lack of understanding is found in many other questions, such as "Is there another world inside our own?" or "Does the Sun have a moon?" Granted that the interior world has a lengthy history, going back at least to the Greek notion of Hades, and the excellent literary source of Jules Verne, but one might have hoped that educational levels had reached the point where the public could recognize how impossible this is.

Many people seem ready, no, eager to be scammed. "Where can I go to buy land on the Moon", or "on Mars", and even worse for those of us who hear the radio advertising, "Where do I go to name a star?" If that isn't bad enough, how about "What's the difference between an astrologist and an astronomist? I would like to become one of them." Maybe I'm too sensitive, but I see that as a triple threat, being ungrammatical, uneducated, and totally insulting.

At least "Do stars get sunburned?" can be answered with mention of complementary heating in close binaries. But I have to admit to shuddering when I read "How many revolutions does the Moon make and how many times does it circle the Earth in one day?" Or for pure madness, "Even though the Sun is a star, why can't we see it at night with the rest of the stars?" Perhaps the answer to that one is that in a planetarium you can see the Sun at night!

Some complain that too many kids are using Yahoo answers to do their homework assignments, but I am willing to bet (or at least pray!)no teacher ever assigned those last three questions. And while I don't know the age of the person who posted the question "When the Moon collides with a star in the sky, what happens to the star?", this is not far from the fourth grade teacher who asked me after a planetarium presentation to her class why astronauts don't bump into stars on their way to the Moon.

Part of the problem, which you may have noted from the Olbers' reference, is that people keep bringing up problems most of us might have thought were solved long ago. In Newton's *Principia,* published in 1673, he explained why rockets work, so we all groan thinking about the ignorant attack Robert H. Goddard suffered from the New York Times in 1920 when the Times said rockets can't work in space. But imagine someone in 2007 still asking "If space is a vacuum, what do rockets push against to get back to the Earth?" I sort of console myself by thinking about Robert Heinlein's story, "It's Great to Be Back!", in which he predicts just that sort of question in an era when there are large, functioning lunar colonies.

Some of the questions seem intelligent, but I have to wonder about what motivates someone to ask "How does Hubble's Law impact society?"

Many of the questions asked leave me totally puzzled. I'm not even certain I understand what some of the posted queries mean, such as "What is the celestial body for Mercury?" And how does one answer "what is the purpose of the other eight planets in the Solar System?" Is the questioner looking for a teleological, theological, eschatological, or philosphical purpose? Yes, I've been asked a similar question a few times at the end of a planetarium show, as I suppose others have. I still don't know how to reply to that one.

All the foregoing does suggest that the information gap between astronomers and the general public is enormous. I fear that the Creation Museum may increase misunderstanding. The creationists are seeking to promote propaganda rather than enhance knowledge and understanding. When even the then head of NASA, a former astronaut himself, can question whether global warming should be addressed, it seems depressingly obvious that politics can play a role in scientific matters four hundred years after Galileo.

I would hope you do not think I am ridiculing the people who post these questions. Some are surprisingly clever notions based on a lack of knowledge that has been long available, and should have been included in everyone's basic education. It is just that astronomy seems to attract so much misunderstanding, although my doctor assures me (with a suspicious glint in his eye) that the public's confusions about health issues are at least as bad.

I cannot offer any easy solutions. Pressuring educators to improve what is taught about our field sounds nice, but I doubt that such pressure would accomplish much. And some people prefer to be self deluded, so we will struggle on, despite those who ask us why we promote the hoax that people ever landed on the Moon. But how do *you* intend to respond to people who saw the creationist planetarium?

WHAT'S A NICE PLANET
LIKE THIS DOING HERE?

What, if anything has happened to Pluto? Did the IAU (International Astronomical Union) really abolish a planet? A lot of hysteria has been spilled over the IAU action, but I think that much of the concern comes from not thinking the matter through, both on the part of the IAU and of its critics.

The IAU has redefined Pluto as a dwarf planet, and thrown into that category a couple of relatively newly discovered objects such as Eris (formerly nicknamed Xena), and the long known Ceres. Eris is actually slightly smaller than Pluto, but Pluto has five moons while Eris seems to have just one.

What about the other (non dwarf) planets? It was recognized even before the space program began exploring them that we have two very different types of objects called planets. Jupiter, Saturn, Uranus and Neptune turn out to be basically giant balls of gas. They are sometimes called gas giant planets or jovian planets. Other characteristics besides low density include lots of moons, rings, and a fast rotation.

By contrast we have Mercury, Venus, Earth and Mars, which are small, rocky, rotate slowly, and have few if any moons. These are often called the terrestrial planets.

A few astronomers have argued that Uranus may actually be something of a transitional form, because it is a bit denser and smaller than the other gas giants. However, it has the stigmata of rings and lots of moons, so I say leave it where it is.

Now of course we also have over 2000 known planets going around other stars. Given the difficulties of discovery, it is no surprise that nearly all of them fall solidly in the jovian camp in terms of size and mass. In fact, a majority are actually heavier than Jupiter. Exactly one has been found, orbiting a pulsar, that is in the range of the mass of Pluto. The same pulsar has three other known planets. Some argue they are remnants of a planetary system destroyed when a star collapsed to form the pulsar.

Regardless, we have been referring to all four objects around the pulsar as planets. When necessary, one can modify the word planet with an adjective—small, large, dense, light-weight, hot, cold, jovian, terrestrial, plutonoid, dwarf, etc.

Some have argued the IAU action was hasty, ill considered, and basically non-representative of astronomical feelings on the matter. The complaint of hasty has some merit, as parliamentary maneuvering had the IAU drop a committee draft proposal that had been worked on for more than a year in favor of something cooked up literally overnight.

The accusation of ill-considered derives from the definition arrived at. This definition explicitly is only for the Solar System, leaving the non-solar planets drifting uncategorized in space. That includes the one around a pulsar that would be a dwarf planet were it around the Sun. The definition is also ridiculed for saying a planet must have cleared minor junk away from its orbit. Of course, Earth, Mars, Jupiter and Neptune share orbital space with asteroids in Lagrangian points, the so-called Trojan asteroids. And Pluto crosses Neptune's orbit. The last time I checked, over 1200 asteroids were known that come close to Earth, suggesting our own planet is far from having cleared its space.

The charge of a non-representative decision comes from the fact that the vote was taken on the last day of an international convention, when well over half the attendees had already left.

So the politics of planetary definitions is as rife with controversy and shenanigans as any other politics or conventions. How to handle it?

First we should admit that the word planet comes to us from ancient times, when the Sun and Moon were counted as planets because they moved in the sky, and the Earth was not a planet. We do not have to lock ourselves into a definition derived from thousands of years ago that may have pleased Ptolemy, but is not in accord with current knowledge.

Current knowledge tells us that there are profound and basic differences between the giant planets and the terrestrial, at least as many as between either of those two and the newly defined dwarf planets. About the only thing they have in common is that they all go around the Sun and are large enough to have a basically spherical shape (and in fact the dwarf planet Haumea is distinctly ellipsoidal).

Perhaps some day we will find true transitional objects, but for now we can make clear cut distinctions. The word planet by itself refers to a large number of objects, which fall into any one of three classes. Under 3500 km diameter, and usually found with a density of 1 to 3 times that of water are the dwarf planets or plutonoids.

With a density of 3 to 5.5 (or more) times that of water and diameters of 5000 to 15, 000 km we have the terrestrial planets.

With a density of 0.7 (or less) to 1.8 times that of water, rotating rapidly, and with diameters of 25, 000 to 150, 000 (or more) km are the giant planets, which presumably includes most of the non-solar discoveries.

Where does this leave Titan, Ganymede and the other large satellites? We could call them captured terrestrials. Triton would be a captured dwarf. Yes, I know theory says they weren't captured (except maybe Triton and our Moon), so the phrase should be captive terrestrials or captive dwarf. The inner solar system would then have five planets, one of them a captive dwarf. Jupiter would hold four captives in thrall, two terrestrial (Ganymede and Callisto) and two dwarf (Io and Europa), along with the more than sixty other moonlets it has.

Our Moon and Miranda (moon of Uranus) are believed to be recombined from collisions that shattered a pre-existing object. In our Moon's case the collision was with Earth, and the bulk of the intruder wound up as part of Earth, our Moon representing just a small surviving fraction. So recombinant objects are another category, our Moon as a recombinant captive dwarf planet, and Miranda a recombinant moonlet.

Are we creating too many categories? I'm not certain. As we learn of more and more objects, classification becomes more complex. I have not even mentioned the rogue category (planets not in orbit around anything), or whether planets accompanying a brown dwarf deserve a separate class. Things were so much simpler when we could just say we want Class M planets.

INTELLIGENT DESIGN

The issue of Intelligent Design, so-called, has been roiling the ranks of science for a decade. Remarks by President Bush have increased the controversy (full disclosure: I am very distantly related to both Presidents Bush). I thought it might be worthwhile to take a look at what is meant by Intelligent Design, and how it impacts astronomy. Scientists in the biological sciences have been the most vocal on the issue, but astronomers are also concerned. At least one professional organization in the field of astronomy has been polling its members on whether and how to take a stand on the subject.

But what is Intelligent Design? It is a concept developed and promoted by the Discovery Foundation's Center for Science and Culture. Both are located in Seattle, WA. The foundation was largely funded by Howard and Roberta Ahmanson, Philip F. Anschutz, and Richard Mellon Scaife. (Only the last of these people was familiar to me before I googled them.) All are extremely wealthy, and all seem to promote conservative Christian or right wing political causes.

Intelligent Design is defined in a report known as the Wedge Document, put out by the Foundation in 1997. It proposes the "overthrow of materialism and its cultural legacies [by] a broadly theistic understanding of nature". To this end it attacks the theory of evolution, claiming that living cells and larger structures are far too complex to have come into existence by the random workings of chance (this is a slightly skewed reading of evolutionary theory). Instead, there must be an intelligent designer behind it all. A major point is that evolutionary theory has some unresolved problems, and therefore should simply be dropped, along with all scientific research on evolution, as Intelligent Design should replace it, since it answers all questions (the Designer did it). Asking why a presumably intelligent designer would include appendices, wisdom teeth, and mosquitoes is not allowed, but this is not seen as a hypocritical evasion, despite the use of some unanswered questions being the basis for the attack on biology.

116

Although the Wedge Document refers to theism (the doctrine that there exists a Supreme Being or Beings), Intelligent Design has been widely presented to school boards, text book selection committees, and even courts, as not promoting a religion. After all, the intelligent designer could be a team of hard working Endoran scientists, or a three headed Znarg from the Lesser Magellanic Cloud, or even a human with a time machine.

One might say this is no doubt all very interesting to biologists and others in the life sciences or paleontology, but why should astronomers care? After all, the Foundation is not claiming Earth is flat, stands still, or is 6000 years old. The concern springs from supporters of Intelligent Design noting that the universe is a very complicated place, subatomic structure is so complex that no one has yet produced a Unified Field Theory, astronomers concede there are details in star formation not yet understood, so therefore . . .

Those who follow science fiction closely remember that as early as 1940 Robert A. Heinlein was predicting that the USA would fall under the control of a theocratic dictatorship. (The idea so upset Heinlein that although he had a title for the story in which this happened, "The Sound of His Wings", he could never bring himself to write it.) One of Isaac Asimov's early stories followed Heinlein's lead, and had an American theocracy ban all scientific research, including space exploration.

Astronomers who have a sense of history will of course remember Galileo's clashes with those who had literalist readings of the Bible. One of these included Joshua commanding "Sun stand thou still" outside the walls of Jericho. If the Earth goes around the Sun, instead of the other way around, then what would be the point of commanding a Sun which does not move to stand still? So far those advocating Intelligent Design have not addressed this Biblical point, although some Islamic figures have described the belief that the Earth is spherical and revolves around the Sun as a grave sin. And there are Christian groups which have for years been circulating a totally false rumor that NASA somehow "found" there are missing days, which exactly match up with Joshua's efforts.

Galileo was not the only scientist interested in astronomy to run into problems with religion. In 1590 Giordano Bruno was arrested, imprisoned for a decade, and finally burned at the stake for the grave heresy of suggesting that the stars had planets around them, and those planets might have life.

Astronomers now date the ages of normal stars reasonably accurately by the amount of hydrogen they have converted to helium, and the rate at which this is being done. Our Sun, for example, works out to about 4.35 billion years old, and is good for another billion years in its current state, after which it will gradually expand into a red giant for a few hundred million years, and then shrink into a white dwarf. Most who believe in Intelligent Design totally reject this entire scenario. The formation of the Sun and planets from nebular material, some stars 13 billion years old, all this is rejected. Astronomy has some unanswered questions, such as dark matter, the cause of the increasing speed of universal expansion, and the origin of the universe. As with biology, unsolved problems are used as a wedge to disqualify everything else astronomers say that those backing Intelligent Design disapprove of.

The Intelligent Design concept has been widely denounced as a back door attempt to get around the constitutional bar on mixing of church and state. Since private and parochial schools are allowed, it is said, those who wish to further religious concepts over science should send their children to such schools, and leave everyone else alone. President Bush presented it as simply allowing equal time for two theories. but this obfuscates the meaning of the word "theory" and begs the question, why not more "theories"? In Hindu cosmology the Earth is shaped like a pizza, riding on the back of an elephant, which stands with one leg on each of four turtles, And the turtles are swimming in an infinite sea. (I was once asked by an Indian friend who had a BA and MA from a university in India, and an MA and PhD from one in this country, why satellites did not bump into the elephant's stomach.) Equal time for the elephant?

Of course, the USA has never been very good about really keeping church and state separate. Years ago I wrote a satirical

SF story looking at a strict separation: http://www.changing thetimes.co.uk/samples/NapWar/love.htm

Those who read it, however, will note that the separation does not end all that well.

In view of the Wedge Document's language, the accusation of a back door entry of religion seems justified, and a "broadly theistic understanding of nature" clearly can impact astronomy. And as has been said by a number of observers, children in Japan, Korea, China, and Europe are learning biology in their classes, not wasting time debating a particular religion's views on the matter. It certainly seems to me that understanding of astronomy will not be enhanced by introducing Intelligent Design to classes. It is bad enough sometimes having to clear students' minds of astrology. And if, in a planetarium presentation to a parochial school class, the teacher jumps up, after some remarks on stellar evolution, and tells the class "that's just the scientists' superstition, we know the truth", the best I could tell myself was that these children would go through life ignorant, and hopefully not wind up in positions of authority.

CHANGING THEORIES

With the recent discovery of a "hot Jupiter" in a triple star system, the idea that triple star systems cannot have a planet would seem to have received the most definitive of all possible refutations: a counter-example. Astronomers, however, should be accustomed to this sort of thing, as the field has lived for centuries with popular and well established ideas that suddenly collapsed upon the presentation of a counter example.

One of the earliest, of course, was that the Earth is flat. Aristotle came up with several proofs that it is spherical (some of them probably "borrowed" from others). He noted that as ships sail away, the hull disappears first, whereas on a flat Earth, the ship would simply shrink in the distance. He also pointed out that travellers to the north found northern stars rising higher in the sky, while those headed south found the northern stars sinking lower. He also noted that the Earth's shadow on the Moon in lunar eclipses always had a curved edge, which only a sphere would create. Aristotle also mentioned that elephants were found in both Morocco—about as far west as the Greeks knew, and in India, as far east as they had gone. With no elephants in the middle (Greece), this proved that Morocco and India were near one another, and when Aristotle's former student, Alexander the Great, got to India, he had nearly circled the Earth. The minor problems with the last example are that we are dealing with two different subspecies of elephant, and going east from India, Morocco is about 15, 000 miles dead ahead.

A few centuries later Ptolemy came up with his infamous theory on planetary motions, involving planets travelling on epicycles, which travelled on deferents, which went around the excentric, which either stood still or went around the Earth. In later centuries it got more complex, until by 1500 there were over eighty motions for five planets, the Sun and Moon. Copernican theory was presented as a way to simplify the math, but it was not until Galileo observed the changing phases of Venus, something the Ptolemaic theory did not permit, that Ptolemy's ideas were shown to be impossible.

William Herschel, one of the greatest astronomers who ever lived, had a few ideas which turned out wrong. He was of the opinion that sunspots are openings in a layer of burning clouds on the Sun, and when we see a sunspot, we are looking through to a cooler object, which might even have life on the surface. About the only correct part is that sunspots are cooler than the rest of the Sun's surface (8500F vs. 9950F).

Another Herschelian theory that had to be abandoned, this time by Herschel's own observations, is that stars come only as single objects, i.e. there are no binaries, triple, etc. Using this assumption, Herschel figured that when two stars appeared next to each other, it was only a coincidence, and he could use such pairings to try to determine stellar distances. Instead, he found that in a few cases one star clearly was orbitting another.

By Herschel's time, astronomers had an approximately accurate idea of the Sun's distance, and hence of how much energy it was producing. Early ideas on how it made this energy (and presumably how other stars made theirs) began, logically enough, with burning, that is, the rapid chemical uniting of carbon and oxygen. Given the rate of energy production and the Sun's mass, if this theory were correct, the Sun would burn out in 30, 000 years. If you reject the idea that the universe was created 6000 years ago, burning can't power the Sun. For a time, some used this argument in the reverse—since the universe is only 6000 years old, burning could work, so don't waste your time looking for another energy source.

In the Nineteenth Century, some astronomers proposed that the Sun was generating energy by shrinking, using the PVT (pressure/volume/temperature)laws that were worked out early in that Century. This extended the Sun's possible life to thirty million years—further back than that, and it would have been larger than Mercury's orbit. But by that time geology was suggesting a far older Earth. Then Madame Curie discovered radium and radioactivity. The Sun clearly was not made of enough radium to energize it. For half a century it was assumed the secret lay somewhere with radioactivity. When Subraman-yan Chandrasekhar finally worked out the equations whereby the Sun converts hydrogen to helium it was after World War 2, and he received a Nobel Prize.

Loads of prominent astronomers and other scientists doubted that space travel would ever be possible. Even an early editor of Astounding Science Fiction magazine is said to have doubted space travel would ever be achieved. Another concept proved wrong.

In 1755 Immanuel Kant proposed the "nebular hypothesis", that the Sun and planets began as a cloud of gas and dust in space. Gravity pulled the cloud together to form the bodies of the Solar System. This theory was widely forgotten, and the Nineteenth Century developed a theory that two stars passed close enough to one another to tear gas out of each. This gas then formed the planets, moons, comets, etc. as it cooled and condensed. Once astronomers learned in 1838 to measure the distance of stars, it could be calculated from their motion just how often these near collisions might occur. The result was that in the entire life of our galaxy, maybe two such events might have occurred, meaning in a galaxy of 200 billion stars, only four stars would have planets. (This idea is impossible—the hot gases would simply have expanded to infinity.)

In the early 1890s American astronomer Thomas Jefferson Jackson See presented evidence suggesting one of the two stars in the 61 Cygni system might be accompanied by a third object. Anyone checking See's numbers would find he was claiming a planet, although he very coolly did not state this explicitly. Since theory suggested few planets, See's results were either attacked or ignored.

Today theories about the formation of planetary systems are much closer to Kant's ideas, although much more complex. In fact, the discovery that over half the planetary systems so far discovered include a "hot Jupiter" again caused the down-fall of a nice simple idea. Our own Solar System approximately increases masses of planets steadily until we get to Jupiter, and then sees a fairly steady decrease. Also, planetary distances seem to roughly double, at least through Neptune, a progression known as Bode's Law. Everyone assumed that when we discovered other planetary systems, there would be small rocky planets near the star, and big, gassy planets far away. But "hot Jupiters" are typically within 2 million to 5 million miles of their stars, much closer than even Mercury is to the Sun. Many are so close that there is some question why they do not simply evaporate in the heat. So farewell to another nice, simplistic idea for planetary systems.

The most modern, up-to-date theory on planetary systems suggests we have four zones around the Sun. The first zone is composed of rocky (silicate) objects with nickel-iron cores: Mercury, Venus, Earth, and Mars. Zone two is the asteroid belt, which itself has a concentration of nickel-iron objects in its inner portion, silicate in the middle, and carbonaceous (like the two moons of Mars) in the outer part. The third zone is made up of the jovian planets, mostly hydrogen with some helium. Furthest out is the Kuiper Belt, whose largest member is Pluto. Objects here are mostly made of ices. To an astronomer, ices include the frozen forms of ammonia, carbon dioxide (dry ice), methane, sulfur dioxide, and water.

But who knows what the theories will say thirty years from now?

Review Requested:
If you loved this book, would you please provide a review at Amazon.com?

OTHER BOOKS BY THIS AUTHOR

FICTION

Time for Patriots: Bunker Hill Confronts the 21st Century
A physics experiment gone wrong sends a military academy back to 1770, where they meet Washington, Franklin, Mozart, and others.

The Mountain of Long Eyes.
27 stories of science fiction, fantasy, satire, horror and humor

ASTRONOMY

Useful Star Names, with Nebulas and Other Celestial Features; 2011
Hundreds of names arranged alphabetically and by constellation, with derivation and meanings where known, Right Ascension and Declination, apparent magnitude, spectral class and distance

Our Neighbor Stars, Including Brown Dwarfs; 2012
The 100 stars nearest Earth, their constellations, Right Ascension, Declination, distance, discoverers, size, temperature, spectral class, planets, and nearest neighboring star. Tables.

Moons of the Solar System; 2013
185 known moons of the planets and dwarf planets, with names, discovery dates and names of discoverers, sizes, orbits, orbital periods, inclinations. Many with photographs from visiting spacecraft.

Impact Craters of Earth, with Selected Craters Elsewhere; 2014

About 200 meteor impact craters are known scattered across every continent of our planet, and even ocean floors. This is the first book ever to describe all of them, giving location, size, and approximate age, as well as the identifying evidence. Some are easily visited, while others are unlikely ever to attract tourists. This book suggests which may be visited or should be avoided. With color photographs of many craters. A few sample craters from elsewhere in the Solar System are included for comparison purposes.

Dwarf Planets and Asteroids; Minor Bodies of the Solar System; 2014

The first asteroid was discovered January 1, 1801. Since then hundreds of thousands have been found. This book presents information on a representative sample, including the first 25 discovered and all those that have been visited by a spacecraft. Discovery dates, discoverers, orbits, periods, sizes, geology, moons, and asteroid families are provided.

Astronomical Numbers; 2016

Hundreds of the most commonly sought or used numbers in astronomy, from the twelve closest stars to the number of both miles and kilometers in a light year and in a parsec, the nearest galaxies, planets' orbits, and brightest stars, the speed of light, eclipses, and brown dwarfs this book is the quickest and easiest reference.

CPSIA information can be obtained
at www.ICGtesting.com
Printed in the USA
FFOW03n1328110218
44944419-45238FF